CONTEMPORARY AMERICAN FICTION

STRAIGHT CUT

At thirty-three, Madison Smartt Bell has published five novels and two collections of short stories, all of them available from Penguin. A native of Tennessee and a graduate of Princeton and of Hollins College, he lives in Baltimore with his wife, the poet Elizabeth Spires.

STRAIGHT CUT

MADISON SMARTT BELL

PENGUIN BOOKS

PENGUIN BOOKS
Published by the Penguin Group
Viking Penguin, a division of Penguin Books USA Inc.,
375 Hudson Street, New York, New York 10014, U.S.A.
Penguin Books Ltd, 27 Wrights Lane, London W8 5TZ, England
Penguin Books Australia Ltd, Ringwood, Victoria, Australia
Penguin Books Canada Ltd, 2801 John Street,
Markham, Ontario, Canada L3R 1B4
Penguin Books (N.Z.) Ltd, 182–190 Wairau Road,
Auckland 10, New Zealand

Penguin Books Ltd, Registered Offices:
Harmondsworth, Middlesex, England

First published in the United States of America
by Ticknor & Fields, 1986
Published in Penguin Books 1987

3   5   7   9   10   8   6   4   2

LIBRARY OF CONGRESS CATALOGING IN PUBLICATION DATA
Bell, Madison Smartt.
Straight cut.
Originally published: New York: Ticknor & Fields, 1986.
I. Title.
[PS3552.E517S7   1987]   813'.54   87–8985
ISBN 0 14 01.5386 1

Printed in the United States of America

ACKNOWLEDGMENTS

This book owes a great deal to Jane Gelfman, Deborah Schneider, and Cork Smith, and without Beth it might not have been written at all.

For Sara Spinelli
and
Jean de La Fontaine

Thus the butterfly had entirely forgotten that it was a caterpillar, perhaps it may in turn so entirely forget that it was a butterfly that it becomes a fish. The deeper natures never forget themselves and never become anything else than what they were.

Søren Kierkegaard,
Fear and Trembling

PART 1 / THE DAY I SHOT MY DOG

THE DOG WAS SUFFERING, mainly from old age. She was twelve, thirteen maybe? I couldn't remember for sure. She was a Doberman, black and tan but going gray now, a brush of white hair running the ridge of her back, which was mounded with knots of muscle and some new lumps which were tumors. My dog had cancer. She was also blind in one eye, and had little taste for life left in her. A vigorous fighter and hunter in her prime, she now lay day-long in front of the stove, on the pad I'd made for her, unable to drag herself up and out, uninterested in doing that.

Once a day I could coax her out for a walk. We'd take a turn around the place, the dog limping badly from a tumor behind her left shoulder but wanting to go. The place had gone to seed too. All the fences were down, almost, but that didn't matter so much, since there was hardly anything to keep in. No more horses; that barn stood empty. In or around the second barn, about a half mile from the house down a little lane and through a couple of broken gates, I still had a few sheep and I'd take the dog with me in the evening to put out a little molasses for them, though they were half wild anyway and didn't particularly care if I showed up or not.

On one of these little outings I was in the feed room dipping a coffee can into the molasses bin, and there was a rat in there, a fat gray one — I stabbed down with the edge of the can without thinking, broke its back but didn't kill it. Now I had a paraplegic rat in the molasses bin, and I couldn't quite bring myself to hit it again, finish it off. This is what I have a dog for, I thought then. I tipped the bin and the rat fell out in the trampled mud in front of the feed room and began trying to drag itself up under the barn, using its front legs only. The dog crippled after the rat, did catch it, did kill it. Then she took it off somewhere to maul it and bury it. Probably that was the most fun she'd had in a year, but a broken-down dog catching a broken-down rat was too much for me to contemplate, and I knew I had to do something.

There were plenty of guns in the house; my father had left them there. When I got back I dug out a rifle and cleaned it and found a box of shells. The dog had stayed out with her rat and sometime after dark I heard her dragging herself up the porch steps, one step at a time. I let her in and she limped over to her pad. I built a fire in the stove for her; it was May and we didn't need it, but she liked a fire.

Do it and get it over with was what I told myself the next morning. I called the dog and she stood up shakily, looking at me and then at the rifle. Her blind eye, the left one, had swelled and turned a light marble blue, and it always seemed to be looking at something, the next world, perhaps, or something else I couldn't see. The sighted eye, a soft gold brown, looked at the gun and said no to it. The dog lay back down and wouldn't get up again, not even when I took the gun and went a little way into the yard, hoping to fool her out of the house that way.

There went another day, and the next day I got a leash on her and got her in the car and drove her off to the vet, something she hated. I parked outside the place and led her into the waiting room, where she skittered around a minute or two on the slick linoleum, legs slipping out from under her right and left, before I persuaded her to sit down. There were a couple of other dogs there with their owners, and it was a measure of her misery that she didn't offer to fight any of them. She just crouched there, trying to sit down and not touch the floor at the same time. I was glad we didn't have to wait very long.

The vet knew me and knew my dog; he'd been treating her for years, and dogs I'd had before, and dogs my family'd had. So when we took her back he didn't even bother putting her up on the table.

"You want her put down" was what he said, a statement not a question. My dog was squatting on the floor against my leg and I could feel her trembling.

"I was going to shoot her myself yesterday," I said. "She saw me pick up the gun and she wouldn't come out with me."

"Gun-shy?"

"Didn't use to be," I said. The vet looked at me for a long time. I'd known him most of my life and now he was getting older too, fifty or fifty-five he must have been. His hair was running back at the sides and a big blue vein had popped out of his forehead and forked over the bridge of his nose.

"This is not something I'm supposed to do," he said finally. "I could lose my license. You know that."

"Oh, that's all right," I said. It was no news. That pernicketiness about where the drugs went was the reason I hadn't wanted to ask. "I'll figure out something." I flicked the leash and the dog got up, looking a little happier than she had been, thinking she might get out of there without anything horrible happening.

"Wait a minute," the vet said, and he left the room and shut the door behind him. It was a very average little cubicle, not much different from a doctor's examining room, with a sink and table but no chairs. There were a couple of tin cabinets on the wall and next to them a faintly humorous print featuring cats. I was looking at that when the vet came back. He had a heavy-duty syringe in his hand with what looked like about ten cc's of some lethal mauve-colored liquid.

"A big muscle's best," he said. "The hip or the shoulder."

"You sure it's okay?" I said. He looked at me; he wasn't going to answer that. I picked up the syringe, which was capped.

"Wait," the vet said. He handed me a little paper sack to carry the syringe out of the office with.

"I appreciate it," I said, and it was true. It had been a long time, I realized in the car, since I'd had a disinterested favor from anyone, though of course that might well have been my own fault.

Back at the house the dog and I went our separate ways till late in the afternoon. Then I went out to the shed beside the house and got a shovel. The dog fell in with me as I started toward the back of the place. She was moving a little better, I thought, stiff but steady, a sort of marching pace. From the lane to the sheep barn I could see the sun dropping down behind the far end of my biggest field, the field green and turgid with spring rain. In her younger days the dog had spent hours running that field, trying in splendidly idiotic wonderment to catch meadowlarks on the wing. My pleasure in the grace of her movement had been almost as great as her own, though of course that wasn't something to think about now.

I threw molasses out for the sheep, with the dog sitting down to watch and panting rather heavily, though it wasn't really very hot. There was a new lamb that day, I just barely noticed. It looked like it would make it without being put up. I went through a gate at the back of the lot and into a sort of thicket that ran up the edge of the hill pasture. The dog followed along at her workmanlike trot. We broke into the open again just above the sheep lot fence and the pond, above the first of the three terraces too. The hill was steep and it had been terraced years before to keep it from washing out altogether.

By the time I reached the second terrace the dog had fallen behind. At the third terrace I had to stop myself. I dropped the shovel and leaned on my knees, panting like the dog. Here in the upper reach of the pasture there were more buckbushes than grass this year. My family had reclaimed this land, and I was letting it go to ruin, but there we are. I climbed more slowly to the brow of the hill, and stopped where the ground leveled off. A few yards farther was another fence and woods ran back from it to the crest of the hill and down the other side. I stopped where I was and began to dig.

The dog was coming up more slowly, stopping now and then to rest and zigzagging across the slope to make the grade easier. She reached me before I was half done with my hole, walked past without interest, and flopped down on her side, a position which made the tumor under her shoulder more prominent. I remembered in spite of myself how fresh-turned earth had once affected her as vividly as a drug.

There'd been a lot of rain so it wasn't hard digging, and I wasn't asking a big hole of myself, just one deep enough to discourage the buzzards. It wasn't long, not really long enough, before I got it three feet deep, and I put down the shovel. The dog was sitting up now and I went and sat cross-legged on the grass beside her. After a moment I drew her head down into my lap and began to rub her ears at the base, which she loved. At the same time, with my other hand, I slipped the big vicious syringe out of my shirt front where it had been riding and jabbed it into her shoulder. The dog shivered a little and looked up at me with her live brown eye and that otherworldly blue one, but she didn't match me with the pain. I was the person that was rubbing her ears, after all. I pushed in the plunger and two seconds later I had a dead dog on my hands.

I sat there for quite some time with the dog sprawled over my lap, and while I was sitting there it got dark. There was an excellent view from the hilltop. Scrub was creeping into the pasture from both sides of the cleared field, and on the southern side the woods ran back out of sight, hiding the road which was my border there. But I was looking down to the west, over the pond with sheep gathered around it no bigger than toys, past the road that bordered two sides of the big front field. There were lights starting to come on in the new tract houses on the other side of the road, creeping toward me, it almost seemed. I looked to the north, over the abandoned horse barn to my own house, an old saltbox, dark. There was a hook of crescent moon up above it and as it got darker there were stars emerging too, out of the fading chalk blue of the sky. After some time, I couldn't have said how long, I shifted the dog's head out of my lap and let her body stretch limp on the grass beside me.

You get over your old dog by getting a new dog, but I understood, sitting there on the hilltop, that I wouldn't have the heart for that this time. I was too washed out, too numb, inert. Getting older might have had something to do with it. Forty hadn't arrived yet but it was in sight. Then you had to start thinking about the halfway point. Considering all that, I shifted the soles of my feet together and pressed my knees all the way out to the ground. Light karate workouts I'd kept up over the years made me still able to do little tricks like that, and it was some comfort when I thought of my age, which I seemed to do more and more often these days. On the other hand my left elbow was permanently wrecked with tendinitis. There'd be no cure for that or for other tribulations the years would be careful to bring my way. Also, my wife had left me five months before, though that was neither unexpected nor catastrophic; the marriage had been a bit on the technical side anyway. What was bothering me, I suppose, was the notion that not soon, but eventually, I'd be as dead as my dog was now. Then I got up and buried her and went back down the hill.

I carried my little black cloud of ennui into the house with me. Nothing had changed since my parents had moved deeper into the country a few years before. The three ground floor rooms and the enclosed porch remained exactly the same in every detail, except that I had wired an answering machine to the wall phone in the kitchen. Next to that on the butcher block counter was a fifth of George Dickel, either half empty or half full, depending on your state of mind. I had begun to associate these two articles together for some reason, perhaps because I had got very little use out of either for the past several months. There was a call on the answering machine when I came in from burying the dog, but I didn't listen to it, nor did I fix a drink.

The kitchen clock let me know it was dinner time or thereabouts, so I went into a brief cooking flurry. I chopped up an eggplant, a bell pepper, a yellow squash, tomatoes, onion and garlic, and threw all of these things into a skillet with olive oil. While it simmered I made myself a glass of ice water and turned on the TV to catch a segment of the evening mayhem, which was much the same as usual. After the local news and the national news the dish was done. I spooned some onto a plate and tasted it. It was good, but I couldn't eat it. I put the food into a plastic pot for the refrigerator and washed the plate and the skillet. It was still very early.

Some sitcom had come onto the tube. I turned it off and went on the porch, where I sat down in an armchair and switched on a light. From the reflection in the small window behind the stovepipe I could ascertain that I still resembled myself when last seen. The second volume of *Either/Or* was lying on top of the bookcase near the chair and I picked it up and opened it to the place I'd stopped last. Kierkegaard on "The Aesthetic Validity of Marriage." I read this: "But the more freedom, the more complete the abandonment of devotion, and only he can be lavish of himself who fully possesses himself."

I liked that. But what followed seemed incomprehensibly convoluted. I sat there for five or fifteen minutes watching the letters crawl around on the page, and finally closed my eyes. It occurred to me that if I drank the rest of the bourbon I'd probably be able to cry, but I didn't get up for it. I hadn't taken a drink since Lauren had left — well, two or three days later maybe — and though it was much like locking the barn once the horse had been stolen, I was still determined not to take one.

So I decided to get up and listen to the message, click, beep, hiss: "This is Kevin calling for Tracy. Give a call back as soon as you can." He mentioned a New York number. There was a little pause. "It's work," he said, and there was another click and beep on the tape, signifying that he'd hung up. I shut off the machine and stood there with my finger on the button, thinking how eerie it was that he'd picked the perfect moment to call. Ordinarily I would have ignored it, or maybe I would have changed my number. But as it was . . .

I sat down on the stool beside the counter and dialed the phone. Kevin picked up on the third ring. At the sound of his voice the hairs on the back of my neck stood up, completely of their own accord. It had been a long time since we'd talked.

"Hello. Hello? Is anybody there?"

"It's Tracy," I said finally, telling myself there was no risk in that much anyway. "Returning your call."

"*Well*," he said. "How've you been? Long time, no hear from, you know." Amazingly genial, he was, just like nothing had ever happened.

"About the same as usual," I said. "What about you?"

"You still like the country life?" he said.

"It goes along," I said. "It pretty much takes care of itself."

"You don't feel a little rusty? You're not stagnating way down there?"

"Not particularly," I said, though given the color of my evening this was perhaps not precisely true. "Why the sudden concern, Kevin?" I was getting back in the swing of it, fencing with Kevin on the phone. It seemed to do something for my adrenal reserves. In fact I'd always liked him quite a bit, even when I hated him.

"Oh," he said. "I thought you might like to travel."

"It's possible," I said, wondering why I'd said it. I didn't want to get involved with Kevin again, ever. Did I?

"Where to?"

"Rome," he said.

"Why don't you start at the beginning," I said, "and finish up at the end."

"Well, it's an edit," he said, "a fine cut. You still cut film, don't you?"

"I still cut film." I reached out, picked up the bottle of bourbon by the neck, and set it down closer to me.

"It's an Italian job," Kevin said. "I'm supposed to give them an editor. They shot over here and they have to cut over there. It's the usual currency regulation bit. So. What's your schedule like?"

"I'd have to check," I said, which was a bald-faced lie. I didn't have anything booked for the next year. "What are you offering?"

Kevin mentioned money, lots of it. About double what I would have accepted.

"Nice price," I said. "Expenses?"

"Of course expenses. You'll take it?"

"What's wrong with this picture?" I said. "Let me think. I get over there, cut their film, they pay me in lire and I'm supposed to carry it out of the country in my shoe."

"No, no," Kevin said. "Nothing like that. You'll get yours at this end."

"Half in advance," I said.

"No problem. But I need an answer right now, really. I'd like you to be there at the end of the week."

I considered. That was two or three days. It could be done. But why was I even thinking about it? It was a lot of money, of course. I didn't need it right away, perhaps, but I could use it, what with property taxes and all. Still, so far, I was only entertaining the idea voluptuously in my mind.

"How about a certified check for the first half?" I said, and waited to see what he'd say to that. Ask me if I trust you, bastard, and the phone will blow up in your hand. He didn't.

"If that's what you want," he said. "You'll do it, then."

"It's such a great deal for me," I said. "What are the fringe liabilities?" I was wondering about that, what it would turn out to be. Any mysterious packages to deliver to guys with no last names, Kevin? But I didn't say that out loud.

"I saw Lauren," Kevin said. "Oh, when was it, sometime last week I think." This was such an adroit change of direction that I forgot my last question till after I'd hung up the phone.

"That's nice," I said. I didn't even know she was in New York, but I wasn't going to tell him that. I unscrewed the cap from the bourbon, smelled it, put the cap back on. Of course I didn't care if they were seeing each other. "You see her again, tell her I said hello."

"I'll do that," Kevin said. "So, you want the job?"

"I'll have to check my book," I said. "Can I call you back?"

"Out," Kevin said. "I have to leave soon, you just caught me." I tried to picture him. Was he standing, sitting? Alone? If someone was with him, was it someone I knew? Paranoia. Though Kevin had his special way of proving your worst fears right.

"Tomorrow, then."

"You should be in New York tomorrow if you want the job," he said. "I'll be home by eight, why don't you drop by? Else it's no go." I think we both tried to hang up on each other at that point, and I suppose you might say we both succeeded.

Did I want a drink or did I want a drink? I reached out my hand and then thought, don't go belting it out of the bottle, that's not the way. Get a glass and some ice at least. Then I decided I'd do it fancy, go out in the field and pick some mint for my drink.

There wasn't enough moon to make much light, and I went stumbling over clumps of uncut grass until my eyes adjusted to the dark. The ground here on the flat was spongy from the rain, and it was pleasantly cool. The mint grew wild in a ditch somewhere about halfway across the field, which I found by tripping into it, soaking myself to the knees.

I picked a handful of broad leaves and a couple of tops for decoration. The fine sweet smell rose from the stalks as I broke them, and it covered both of my hands. I tore a leaf and chewed it on my way back toward the house. It was a quiet night. No drunk teenage drivers for me to pick out of my fence, not yet anyway.

I thought I might not want a drink anymore once I'd had my healthy little walk, but I was wrong, I did. In fact I wanted two big drinks, but not more, and I didn't have any more. Tomorrow was going to be a busy day, what with all the traveling I'd have to do.

AS IT WORKED OUT I slept on the couch that night and woke up with first light, a bit stiff here and there because the nights were still cool. I went out and sat on the bricks below the porch and stretched for a few minutes and then went farther into the yard. There had been a heavy dew, and the grass was cool and wet under my bare feet. I stood in the yard and did twenty front kicks and twenty side kicks and fifty twist punches, wincing a little whenever my left elbow popped. It was getting warmer, and I worked up a light sweat. When I was done with the workout I sat down to stretch and breathe. It pleased me that I didn't seem to have any hangover from the drinks the night before.

There were birds singing invisibly in the trees and a couple of volunteer chickens, banties, came wandering across the yard in front of me, picking at the weeds and dandelions. I had not yet cut the grass this spring, so it was overgrown; also the weeds were taking over. At the lower end of the yard I could see what looked like the beginnings of thistles. These were matters I couldn't seem to bring myself to address. Living here alone, I had wanted to touch nothing, change nothing, as if my mind were repeating endlessly the phrase *don't change, don't change,* while my *self*, whatever that might be, remained in some quiet state of suspended animation. Yet the land was changing anyway, if only by decomposing, on its way, perhaps, toward becoming some new thing. I'd been idle for six months and it was time for me to make some sort of move. Kevin had been right or close when he guessed at that, though I didn't much care to admit it. But it wasn't just Kevin, it was Darwin's rule: you change or die.

There was a tenant house at the far end of the place with a man in it I let live there rent free in exchange for counting the sheep now and then when I was out of town, and things like that. I went into the house and called him and found out he would drive me to the airport. Then I had a shower and packed, light, a few clothes in one shoulder bag and a couple of books and the *American Cinematographer Manual*. By noon I was standing around in the Nashville airport, a good hour early; my flight was at one-fifteen. I thought of spending the time in the bar, but instead I opted for pacing in front of the big wall of windows in the main waiting room, watching planes drop down out of the mild haze to land and smoking too many cigarettes. There wasn't so much as a thought on my mind.

I'd brought a couple of Kierkegaards along in case I felt like getting serious and improving my mind and morals on the plane, and I also picked up a mystery while I was hanging around the airport, in case I got really bored. However, I didn't read on the plane. For half an hour I looked out the window. The plane leveled off in a sunny spot and there was a big fluffy cloud bank below it. Childishly I imagined how much fun it would be to get out and walk around on the clouds, with some sort of helium snowshoes perhaps. It looked perfectly possible, from inside the plane.

When that fantasy paled, I got down to the real business of the trip, rationalization. The mere fact that I was going to

New York, I kept telling myself, didn't necessarily mean that I would take Kevin's offer and go on to Rome or wherever else he might have in mind. Nobody was making me do that, and there were so many beautiful arguments against it. If I didn't take the job, I'd be out a plane ticket at the very worst. There were plenty of other trees I could shake in the city, and in fact it was high time that I shook a few. So maybe I wouldn't even call Kevin. Let him wonder whatever happened to me. Or I could just see him socially, so to speak. Or I could call him for a drink or dinner and talk about the job and try to fox out what was funny about it and then decide. Or, or, or . . .

I was still running around in this squirrel cage when the big gray poisonous cloud that usually covers New York materialized just off the right wing. My heart sank. Why would I want to go to such a place as this? I asked myself, by no means for the first time. The plane dropped through the smog cover and began to bank over the Hudson. Looking down the wing, I could see the buildings of Manhattan, as tidy and neatly defined as an architect's model. I could cover up neighborhoods I'd once lived in with the tip of my finger. Then the plane leveled out and flew over the island to La Guardia.

I could have taken a cab, but I didn't. I waited on the sidewalk for the Q-33, paid my ninety cents exact change, and rode jouncing and rattling in the bus to Jackson Heights, the terminal stop. There I bought a couple of tokens and went down the stairs to the F train. People hummed by me like bullets on the stairs and the platform. I wasn't readjusted yet to the New York forty-mile-an-hour forced-marching pace. On the train I sat with my bag in my lap, watching people covertly out of the corner of my eye.

At 14th Street in Manhattan I got off the train. There was a Puerto Rican junkie bebopping around at the head of the stairs, with a couple of fresh-looking cuts on his face and forearms. As I passed him, he said to himself or the world at large: "Jesucristo, I fucking bleeding to death and I don't even know I'm bleeding . . ."

Perfect. I was back in New York. Sixth Avenue: a heavy smell of roasting meat on the air from the souvlaki stands. On the east side of the avenue a sizable crowd milled through the open junk markets that lined 14th Street. It was six-thirty, two hours before I had planned to call Kevin, if I called him. I wanted him to wait and wonder for at least thirty minutes. I hadn't had a drink on the plane and I thought I would reward myself by having one now — the old familiar doublethink coming back again. I decided to go to Grogan's and see if Terry was still there.

The bar was just off the corner of Seventh. I walked in holding my breath; I was always afraid after a long absence that Terry might be dead or gone when I came back. In fact, nothing had changed; I might have been there just yesterday. It was a long narrow railroad bar, with an unused, atrophied steam table rusting quietly near the door. The bar itself was lined with late-middle-aged blue-collar types, both male and female, black and white, all heavy drinkers and smokers. The place was rank with a smell of old beer and old tobacco and a faint overlay of urine. There were televisions up near the ceiling at each end of the bar, and in the back there were many broken-down booths and tables, some with people sleeping in them.

I found a seat near the end of the bar beside two elderly white ladies with bandannas on their heads.

"Jaysus, Terry, it stinks in here," one said as the bartender came by. "Get a mop and clean the floor."

Terry snarled at her wordlessly and smacked a double shot glass down on the bar in front of me. He was a great burly Welshman, with a battered boxer's face and a wonderful head of silver hair. I'd have guessed him to be around seventy, at least. Terry splashed I. W. Harper into my glass and went off to draw me a beer. I never had to order a drink in this place, it just arrived. When he came back with the beer he mumbled something and I mumbled something. Neither one of us had ever understood a word the other said. We loved each other.

I drank my shot, had a sip of beer, lit a cigarette. No immediate effect. While finishing the beer I began to watch the news on the TV to my left. An experiment on rats had just proved that cocaine was addictive, to the amazement of all. I pushed my two glasses over the little lip on the inside of the bar and Terry came by and refilled them, paying himself from the small pile of singles I'd put up on the bar. I drank the shot. A small effect. The two old ladies got up and left. I read the clock in the mirror, a skill I'd first picked up in this very place. Time was passing.

A man in a white coat was working his way down the bar. When he reached me he pulled two cellophane-wrapped steaks out from under the coat and offered them to me for three dollars. It seemed like a bargain, but I declined. Terry came back and poured me a free drink, pumping the bourbon bottle like a salt shaker.

"Thanks." I said.

He walked away without saying anything. An old black man sat down on the stool to my right and began hissing something into my ear. I couldn't understand him and I didn't much want to. He smelled like he might have been dead for three days. I turned the other way on my stool and drank my free shot. There was a muscle-bound white truck-driver type with a Cat hat on sitting at the corner of the bar to my left and staring rather unpleasantly in my direction. I swiveled back to the center and looked at myself in the mirror, the image of my face balanced on the necks of bottles on the shelf behind the bar. Light reflected from my glasses so that I couldn't see my own eyes. That was pretty tough looking, or so I thought. Various New York phone numbers I knew began to play themselves back in my head.

Then the old black man and the Cat hat were in a fight. Terry came quickly around the end of the bar. I stood up. I could move if I needed to. Terry grabbed each man with one hand by the throat and jerked them apart. It was like a man breaking up a dogfight. He dragged them to the door and threw them both out and stood in the doorway screaming after them in some language incomprehensible to me — Gaelic, perhaps. I sat back down and reached for my beer.

Now there was a game show on TV. Terry came back behind the bar and poured himself something black from an unmarked bottle and filled up the glass with Coke. He knocked back half of it, whatever it was, and lit a cigarette.

"What's that you're drinking?" I said. I had to rephrase the question several times before he understood it.

"Blackberry brandy," he said.

"Jesus," I said. I clicked my glasses together and got another drink. I watched the game show through two commercials. Then I read the clock in the mirror. It was seven-forty. I'd drunk enough to be confident, but not enough to be stupid, or so I hoped. I went to a pay phone on the wall opposite the bar and called Kevin and told him I'd be by in ten or fifteen minutes. When I came back to the bar Terry had poured me another free one, and I drank that quickly before I left.

When I hit the street I was feeling good, feeling fine, feeling no pain whatsoever. The drinks had given me a nice little buzz, without stupefying me. I walked over to Ninth Avenue and headed up into Chelsea, where Kevin lived. It was a mixed neighborhood over here, with a lot of Spanish. People were out on the steps with radios and beer and joints. Summer in the ghetto was gearing up.

I turned left on 19th Street. The lights were out on the block for some reason. Two shadows fell in hard behind me as I turned the corner. I just had time to drop my bag before they had me, one clamping his arms around my body from behind and the other with a knife just under the point of my chin, pushing my head up and back, the blade piercing the skin a little, or at least that's what it felt like.

"Easy," I said. "You definitely got me, gentlemen. The

wallet's in the back pocket." I only had about thirty dollars cash, anyway.

The one with the knife reached around the back and pulled my wallet. Then he went in my front pocket and found my money clip, which was a present from Lauren. Damn. He stepped back a little to see what he had.

"Let's be reasonable about this," I said, feeling a little bolder with the knife off my neck. "Take the cash and give me back the other stuff, you'll never move it anyway."

The man in front cracked me one across the face with the back of his hand. Gratuitous, that was. I blinked and looked at him. He had my wallet open and was thumbing through the cards, holding the knife against the back of the wallet like a bookmark or something. I got off a front snap kick, hitting him in the crotch with my instep, lifting him a couple of inches off the ground, then twisted and drove my elbow back hard into the ribs of the one behind me and at the same time hooked a spear thrust over my own shoulder into his eye. He let go and I spun out and hit him over the kneecap with a side kick. He went down. Couldn't believe I'd made that shot; I was never very good at spinning kicks. The one in front was lying on his side throwing up. I picked up my stuff from the ground, and the knife too, and then I ran.

In Kevin's entryway I waited for five minutes before I could stop shaking. Another drink would have gone down good but I didn't have one handy. It was amazing I'd been that stupid. I could have lost my life over a clip and a couple of pieces of plastic. What was really riskier, I wondered suddenly, a straightforward mugging or a quiet, tricky little evening with Kevin? Lucky me, I was getting a chance to try both and compare. Finally I calmed down enough to ring the bell.

When Kevin opened his door I felt immediately that rush of excitement, affection, and (yes) trust, all part of the symbiosis that characterized our better moments together. Knowing full well that Kevin had charmed countless other people, often to their ruin, I still told myself at times that it went deeper than that, still believed he loved me too. I had not seen him in the flesh for several years. We gave each other a big hug and back slap and stepped apart, each instantly wary; in retrospect I can see that he may have had even more excellent reasons for caution than I.

"Hey, you've cut yourself" was the first thing he said. "You're bleeding."

I touched my chin and my fingers did come away red. "I nicked myself shaving this morning," I said. "I must have brushed it on the way over."

Being around Kevin inspired me to tell lies about the littlest things. I stepped around him and went into the bathroom. It wasn't much of a cut, I could see in the mirror, but it seemed to be a bleeder. I washed it with cold water and pressed a Kleenex over it to stop the bleeding. While I was waiting for it to quit I took the knife out of my pocket and flicked the slide. Six inches of double-edged steel came rattling out, *zot*, straight out of the handle, not jackknifing like an ordinary switchblade. Under my index finger, the blade felt very sharp indeed. I pushed back my sleeve and tried it on my forearm; it gave a closer shave than the razor I used on my face. You could just nudge the thing up against somebody and be in his carotid artery with a touch of your thumb. Vicious little mother. I pushed the slide the other way and the blade sucked back into the handle.

Kevin's loft was basically one big room laid out on an ell with the short end at the front door. There was a sort of sleeping compartment built into the other end of it. The walls were white and lined with modestly framed stills from various pictures Kevin had had something to do with. He was a fairly good amateur photographer, and had taken most of the stills himself.

I walked down the row of pictures, stroking the cut on my

chin with my thumb. Kevin was sitting at a round Formica table at one end of the loft, under a row of dark uncurtained windows. I sat down across from him. Some people were of the opinion that we resembled each other, though he was dark and I was fair, or were negative images of each other, perhaps. The truth was that there was not much of a likeness when you really looked, except for our being about the same build, tall and fairly lean (I was just a little bigger). Kevin's features were sharper and finer than mine, and unlike me he'd put on no weight at all with the years. He also still had all his hair, though it was going gray around the temples.

"Have you eaten?" Kevin said. "You feel like going out?"

"Let's go for a drink," I said. I had an urgent wish to play the next couple of moves on my own territory. Kevin wasn't much of a drinker, as a rule, and he'd been known to get a little careless when he did drink. We strolled over to the Empire Diner, talking idly and harmlessly about the more unimportant members of our mutual circle of acquaintance. It was warm enough for us to sit at the little wrought-iron tables on the sidewalk outside the place. I ordered two margaritas. Kevin liked designer drinks.

They made pretty good margaritas at the Empire, but it could just as well have been straight Sterno for all I cared. I was still a bit jangled from the mugging — attempted mugging rather. My drink was gone in two good hits, and Kevin was fidgeting with his. Not good.

"Drink up, son," I said. "Don't play with it."

Crude, but it worked, Kevin laughed, a little nervously I thought, and finished his glass. I ordered two more and some extra salt. The waiter brought a cutting board with a mound of coarse salt on it. Very nice.

Kevin took an envelope out of his jacket and slid it over the little ironwork diamonds of the table to me. I dropped my hand on top of it.

"Why don't you tell me a little more about this deal?" I said.

"Oh well," Kevin said. "It's pretty simple. Documentary. It's about drug rehab."

"Nice," I said. "Friends of yours?" Couldn't resist. He ignored it, however.

"It's for RAI," he said.

I nodded. That was the Italian state TV network. I'd worked for them, tangentially, before. So had Kevin.

"See, they've still got this heavy heroin problem over there," Kevin said. "So these people set up the project around that." Here Kevin dropped a few names. "They shot at some rehab centers in the city and a couple of them upstate. Behavioral therapy is where they're all at . . . Anyway, it's only an hour program. You could cut it in a month. Less if you're as fast as you used to be. In and out, easy money."

"Ratio?"

"Six to one, maybe a little less."

"Sure," I said. Kevin had possibly just made a little mistake. A six-to-one shooting ratio didn't really agree with such a fancy price for an editor. I opened the envelope. A certified check, by God and Jesus. On Manufacturers Hanover. They were still solvent, so far as I knew. Kevin was two-thirds down his drink. I'd been mousing around with mine. That was more like I wanted it. I stuck my fingers in the salt and licked them. If I could get Kevin a bit drunker it was conceivable he might drop another card. I put the check back on the table.

"I booked you a flight," Kevin said. "Seven P.M. tomorrow. Kennedy."

The waiter came by and I ordered more drinks. What's wrong with this picture? I wasn't playing the game. The game was playing me.

"I don't get it, Kevin," I said. "Why is it so much money?" Sometimes, when subtlety fails you, you can get somewhere with a direct question. Not this time, however.

"Oh well," Kevin said. "The rough cut's pretty rough, actually."

"It'd have to be," I said. "That's not the reason, is it, baby?"

Already it was time for another margarita. I ordered us a couple. Kevin was beginning to look just a little wobbly around the neck, but he still had his mask on straight.

"I was thinking of bumping you onto another job if you were interested," Kevin said. "It would be a trip to Brussels if I can work it out."

"I still don't quite get it," I said. "You're not famous for paying for maybes."

"Oh, it's a pretty good budget on the RAI thing," he said. "Besides, who knows, maybe I owe you one. But I could always pay you less if you prefer."

"No, that's okay," I said. I picked up the check and put it in my pocket. Why was I doing this? Why did the chicken cross the road? Screw it. I seemed to be getting drunk.

"Oh yeah," Kevin said. "Lauren says hello back, by the way."

I looked at him. My, they were seeing a lot of each other. She was sleeping with him again; I could practically smell it. Kevin looked like he was going to go on with the subject. I put my hand on the knife in my pocket. If he started some sort of weird confessional about Lauren I could always jump across the table and slit his throat. No, no good. Get caught for sure.

And now Kevin was running down names and numbers of people in Rome. I took out my book and wrote down all the information. Circumstantial evidence indicated that I'd taken this job. Then we were sitting there over our half-empty glasses, without another word to say to each other.

"So," Kevin said. "Bon voyage, I guess." He looked at his watch.

I pulled the knife out of my pocket and hit the slide. *Zot!*

"Jesus, what's that?" Kevin said.

I was crazy. Too many drinks, and a bit of trouble focusing my eyes. I looked down my nose at the point of the knife and saw Kevin's face somewhere beyond it.

"Present for you," I said. I thunked the knife into the cutting board where the salt had been. It went in an easy inch, like the wood was butter, and shivered when I took my hand away.

"Gee whiz," Kevin said. "What did I do to deserve a nice present like that?"

"Let's say you pay the tab," I said. Not a great exit line, but the best I could come up with on short notice. I got up and touched Kevin lightly on the shoulder and started walking away down Tenth Avenue, no particular destination in mind. Two or three blocks, and I remembered that it's bad luck to give someone a knife. You're supposed to give a penny back to ward it off, and Kevin hadn't done that. Of course, I did have my certified check in my pocket. But somehow I don't think you can buy out a superstition with a check.

5

ACK AROUND 14th Street somewhere I walked into a pizza stand and had a slice of Sicilian with a double handful of plastic mushrooms on it and a vicious cup of coffee, about two days old. I was hoping that the big wad of crust might soak up some of all that bourbon and tequila, and it seemed to work. My brain began to come back. And I began to conjure up ideas for getting off the street.

I still had the master lease on an apartment in Brooklyn. The place was sublet, but I kept keys and couch privileges there, though I was supposed to give more than five minutes' notice before I showed up. The man in the place was a slight acquaintance, but I didn't feel much like chatting with him at present. I was strung up fairly tight from the meet with Kevin, and I needed time to uncoil. It was only a little after ten, and I thought I'd rather not go to Brooklyn until there was a more realistic chance that my subtenant might be asleep.

That left me two or three hours to kill, and I knew it would be better not to spend the time drinking, though naturally that was an early thought to cross my mind. No, the thing to do was try to visit someone, preferably someone who was innocent of any knowledge of or acquaintance with either Lauren or

Kevin. There were several possibilities. I went to a phone booth across the street from the pizza stand and started dropping change. Two no answers, one machine, and then I had Ray, of Harvey and Ray, live and in person at the other end of the line. They were both home and reasonably willing to be dropped in on.

Harvey and Ray's loft was practically a carbon copy of Kevin's, leaving out location and details of decoration. It has often occurred to me that all New York artists' lofts may well have been designed by the same minimalist moron, though I suppose if that was the case somebody would have burned him at the stake by this time. Their place was down at the west end of Prince Street, an easy distance from numerous hot spots around the Village and the waterfront, but I don't think either one of them cruised much anymore. Harvey and Ray seemed to stick together better than a lot of straight couples I knew, though I can't say that I knew them terrifically well.

Both of them were actors, not terribly famous or successful, but they got by. They did bit parts in plays and movies, and quite a bit of TV commercial work for the rent and sushi money, which latter fact had caused us to blunder across each other at parties fairly frequently, a couple of years back when I still lived in the city. Harvey was a bit of a camera buff, and he liked to talk to technicians, and he used to have me to dinner once in a while to pick my brains about different equipment he was interested in. Both of them were excellent cooks, so it was an even trade.

The walk down had cleared my head to some degree. Harvey and Ray were drinking Pernod when I got there, but I passed on that and went for a glass of ice water. The opening chitchat seemed to run out fairly quickly, and as I sat in what was dragging into a rather sticky silence, I began to wonder if dropping by here had been a mistake. They weren't people I usually burst in on without warning; it was late enough to be weird; I might have interrupted something . . .

"Oh," Harvey said then. "I got film from our trip." One of the catch-up details they'd told me was that they'd been to Italy in April. "You want to watch it?"

"Sure, set it up," I said, hoping they hadn't seen me cringe. Like most amateurs, Harvey was infinitely more interested in the equipment itself than in anything he could possibly do with it. On the other hand, the films of his I'd seen before were as good or better than Thorazine for blunting the sharp edges of a troubled mind. The mood I was in, that might not be so bad, and it would certainly kill time. Harvey was bustling around with a projector and a screen. I knew he would flak me about in-camera editing, which I know nothing and care less about, but I had survived that before.

Ray shut off the light, and here came the fresh marvels from Harvey's latest super-8 wonder box. Italy. Well, I would be there in about thirty hours, after all. Maybe I could learn something.

Picturesque natives in the Piazza Navona, the Washington Square of Rome. A shot of Ray walking past the Bernini fountain there.

Exteriors of several Roman churches. The courtyard of St. Peter's: Harvey and Ray together, arms linked; the shot taken by some cooperative bystander, possibly the pope.

A big bird's-eye view of Vatican City, shot from the dome of St. Peter's, I would guess. Then Harvey in close-up, framed against the sky. Harvey had the sort of looks advertisers like to call rugged. He wasn't a bad-looking guy. Ray, on the other hand, was more the Woody Allen type, though he brought home a lot of bacon playing klutzy roles in commercials: the guy who can't handle washing the dog and so forth. He practically worshiped Harvey's beauty. The shot held for a long time.

"That would make a nice head shot," I said, for the sake of moving my mouth.

"Oh no, never," Ray said. Such modesty.

"Don't know how it would print," Harvey said. The reel

ran out and Harvey got up and loaded another one. I could see that there were plenty more, enough to last me till time to go home, easy.

Venice. Ray propped in the bow of a gondola in a sort of sultan's pose, laughing. Harvey in the Piazza San Marco with pigeons sitting all over him.

More of much the same.

The third reel: Florence. Ray contemplating the Michelangelo slave sculptures. A jouncing shot across the Ponte Vecchio. What seemed to be a communist rally in front of the Uffizi, red rags in abundance and much gesticulation. My God, these two had the luck of fools and little children. I didn't think tourists were supposed to film things like that.

Florence from the Belvedere. Here my interest was somewhat roused. The view of the city was magnificent from the old fort; also, I had certain associations. Harvey had done a more tolerable job than usual on a long slow pan over the city. He seemed to be using a tripod for once, or maybe he'd braced his arms on the wall. The city moved slowly through the frame from right to left. At around a hundred eighty degrees the shot flicked briefly over a knot of people who must have been up on the Belvedere with Harvey, so close they were out of focus. Harvey panned around to San Miniato on the hill behind and zoomed in on the façade.

"Wait a second," I said. "Can we run that back?" Ten thousand hours of editing gives you a certain responsiveness to the subliminal.

"You like that one?" Harvey said. He was rewinding the film.

"It's worth seeing twice," I said. There, I'd squeezed out another compliment. Here came the pan again. Ninety degrees. One twenty. One seventy. I leaned forward.

There. Extreme close-up, a hair too close for the depth of field. Lauren. On screen for possibly a third of a second, and gone. Two degrees to the right and in slightly better focus: Kevin.

On to San Miniato. I sat back in my chair.

"Would have been a nice one if those people hadn't walked through it," Harvey said.

"Oh, I don't know about that," I said.

"Huh?" Ray said.

"It's an interesting effect," I said. Utter foolishness, but since I was supposed to be the expert I could get away with it. The effect on me personally was certainly interesting enough. The next hour of film clips was absolutely meaningless. I had regressed to the point where I couldn't read the image, couldn't resolve the lines and shadows on the screen into representations of anything at all.

Around midnight they ran out of film and put the lights back on. I looked at my watch, faked surprise and dismay at the time, and said good-bye, not too abruptly I hoped. When I got back to the street I was stone cold sober, which had been part of the plan. Otherwise, the scheme of cooling out with Harvey and Ray might fairly be said to have backfired.

That being the case, I decided to walk to Brooklyn. It was a straight shot east to the bridge, and at that time of night I had an even chance of beating the train. I hitched up my bag and started across Prince Street. At West Broadway I crossed down to Spring.

Most immediately on my mind was the infamous chicken theory of the cinema. Marshall McLuhan thought it up, and it goes more or less like this: Some anthropologists go to the jungle with their movie cameras and wander until they find an appropriately pristine tribe of natives. They make friends and spend weeks filming the normal activities and special ceremonies of this tribe. All goes well.

The anthropologists depart to process, cut and print their film; then they return to show it. With native helpers they construct a special hut for the screening. Night falls, the tribe assembles, and the show begins. And ends.

The natives are singularly unimpressed. In fact, they seem quite bored.

"Well, how did you like the movie?" say the anthropologists, or words to that effect.

"What are you referring to?" the natives inquire.

"Why, *you*," the anthropologists say. "Your daily lives, hunting, farming, dancing, and so forth. Yourselves, up there on the screen."

"The august visitors must be crazy," the natives say. "There was nothing on the screen but lights and shadows."

At this point the anthropologists become annoyed. They barricade the hut and announce their intention to run the film again and again, until *someone* sees *something*.

Which they do. The film is run and rerun many times.

At last a perspicacious native raises his hand. The anthropologists stop the film and ask with some excitement what he has seen.

"I saw a chicken," the native says.

The anthropologists are now, if possible, even more perplexed and annoyed than before. So far as they know, there are no chickens in this particular shot: a big village dance scene full of activity. But the native insists that he saw a chicken and nothing more. The anthropologists adjourn the screening and examine the relevant section of film on hand rewinds. At length they discover that a chicken does indeed appear on about twelve frames of the film, for approximately half a second, deep in the shot and obscured by two lines of vigorous masked dancers, scurrying between two huts in the background.

So the anthropologists gather the natives again and once more they screen the film. The native who originally saw the chicken still sees the chicken, in the precise spot where the anthropologists now know that the chicken is located, and he sees nothing more.

They run and rerun the film. Eventually more natives begin to see the chicken, and only the chicken. Then they begin to perceive other isolated and improbable items until they are seeing the entire movie. At last, they have been successfully initiated into a whole new culture of illusion.

But what does it all mean? No one knows for sure. Though the legend has it that all commercially successful films in the West do have a chicken in them somewhere; be it only for half a second . . .

An apocryphal story, in all probability. But I like it. So much so that I kept telling it to myself, elaborating the details over and over, all the way east, across the long, barren, and ever so slightly dangerous section of Delancey Street just before the bridge. Then up the stairs and the first interminable leg of the walkway, still pushing, still rehearsing the chicken theory, until I reached the center of the main span, where I felt that I could stop. After drinking so much and walking so far, I had to be in control. Downhill the rest of the way, and I had pushed myself up within sight of the limit of my physical endurance, my shoulder bag growing a little heavier with each step, as though it had translated into weight the thousand-odd miles I'd traveled so far that day and the few thousand more I'd travel tomorrow. The walkway was even more dilapidated than it had been the last time I'd been up there, and at the place where I stopped the rail was broken off on the north side, so that with a good running start I might have cleared the roadway and landed just in the wake of that tug and barge shoving slowly up the East River, to sink and perhaps be dissolved in the poisoned water even before I could drown.

If I wanted to. But I didn't care for that or for anything else in particular, except for a quietus to be set upon my consciousness. To not think of possible applications of the chicken theory, so beautiful in the abstract, to my own predicament. To not consider that, of the long procession of images I had witnessed, only the presence of two people, however fleeting, had made the whole thing visible for me. That of the two, I could not tell which one had made the image real and brought the monster of memory back up whole and alive into my life.

FLORENCE from the Belvedere. It is no more possible truly to describe a landscape than it is to describe a face. And if a landscape such as that, or any other, were by some miracle to discover a mouth and speak for itself, it would have such a burden of history to unfold that it would not be done with it before the end of the world. But for my own little story, the scene was not much more than a background.

That would have been ten or twelve years back, the time of one of the first "Italian jobs" I did with Kevin. I had left Rome to take a break from the singular madness of Italian movie making, and in Florence I had walked across the river and out of the city to seek relief from the confusion of an ununderstood language (I spoke only about ten words of Italian at the time, whereas now I speak almost thirty) and also to get away from the tourists; it was the height of the summer season and all Italy was thronged with them.

Owing to this set of circumstances I stumbled up into the Belvedere, at the end of a long walk through the gardens below. I had not known the place was there and I found it by complete accident, but once I had arrived I liked it. The view, as I have mentioned, is spectacular, and the steep ascent discourages most tourists, though there is a road running up the back of the hill. There were some sightseers I had to share the hilltop with, but not too many of them.

I stood for ten or fifteen minutes by a parapet overlooking the city, luxuriating in the panorama, and then began to walk slowly around the inside of the walls. I was walking clockwise, and Lauren, whose name I did not yet know, was walking counterclockwise. In this way we passed each other about five times. Each time I looked at her, glanced at her, she kept looking better and better.

On the sixth pass she spoke.

"Are you following me?"

We'd both been up there an hour at the least. Lauren was speaking French. I replied in some semblance of the same tongue.

"No. But it would be a great temptation to do so."

I walked on; she walked on. This was almost all the French I knew.

Eventually I sat down on one of the outer parapets. I thought that she would probably return that way, since it was the direction which led to the city. I had my back to where she must be, however. I was very casual. I smoked a cigarette, then another, looking out at the profile of the Duomo. A hand touched me in the small of the back and I almost fell in the river. I just barely saved myself by locking my legs hard around the wall.

So much for my savoir-faire. When I collected myself enough to look around I saw Lauren a few paces away, cracking up. She was laughing like a loon.

"What's your favorite language?" I said, expending the very last of the French I had in store. It turned out to be English, luckily or unluckily for me.

Lauren was an extraordinary beauty, in truth and fact and without prejudice, the sort that grows on you slowly and never quits. Others of her admirers compared her to the works of Botticelli, and the simile was not without justification, though it got old fast, especially when it was suggested by persons other than myself. But Lauren did share the fine lines, the clear articulation of feature, specifically of the Botticelli Venus, which was enshrined in the Uffizi just down the hill and across the river. Though Lauren was considerably less vapid than the girl on the half shell there. She wasn't a goddess; she was a woman, and her humanity added a great deal to the lines Botticelli might have drawn and most certainly would have admired. It made her more beautiful and more dangerous as well, much more so in both cases than any painting could ever be.

I learned, those first few days in Florence, not much at all about Lauren. So far as her own taste ran, the outward circumstances of her life were utterly without interest or importance. I did learn that she was a British citizen but had spent most of her childhood on the Continent, mainly in Switzerland; she was the second daughter of a diplomatic family. She had an undergraduate degree from Radcliffe, had been to acting school in New York, and did occasional modeling work. Her passport listed a London address. At the time that I met her, Lauren was twenty-two.

Lauren's Italian was very good and she knew Florence much better than I did. For two days she conducted me on an unorthodox tour of the city, disappearing a trifle mysteriously at the end of each evening; she would not allow me to escort her home. On the third night she came back with me to my hotel, though I had not suggested it. There, for two or three more nights, we shared a smallish bed, without touching, as though there were a sword between us. I won't say that I was shy, just curious to see what she would do if I left her to her own devices. It's also possible that my subconscious early warning system was already in effect. It was she who turned to me when we made love for the first time.

When I had to return to Rome at the end of the week, Lauren accompanied me, quite as if it had all been planned in advance. I had not invited her; I did not object to her coming. Her suitcase, as it turned out, was already checked at the station.

Lauren and Kevin were immediately intrigued with each other, a development which I had anticipated. After a week's absence from the cut, I was very busy, and Kevin, the producer, was relatively idle; he'd come over mainly for the trip. So it was natural that Lauren should spend more time with Kevin and less with me while I put in ten- and twelve-hour days on the flatbed, cutting a none-too-interesting program on the then New York art scene. Most nights Lauren returned to my room, occasionally not. I'm not sure exactly which day she and Kevin closed the triangle. At the time I thought I didn't care.

I was nearly seven years older than Lauren, so I had an edge on her in experience (though there's always the theory that women of her kind know everything from the instant of their birth). My love life at that time centered on avoiding inconvenience; you may say that I was just a little jaded. Lauren was an enormous refreshment to me, but I was determined not to let her become any more than that. From the very beginning I knew it would be unwise to be in love with Lauren, and for a long time I believed that I was not.

For all of these excellent reasons I was undisturbed, maybe even relieved, when Kevin took Lauren back to New York with him, leaving me to wrap the edit and also some other tricky business that was going forward under the table. So far as I was concerned, she was well out of my way. It's also true that in those days I was closer to Kevin than I had ever been to any woman, or ever expected to be.

And more than a decade later, it was still frustrated love for Kevin, not Lauren, that could spoil my sleep, at one point bouncing me all the way out of the couch before I could even locate myself, back in the old apartment in Brooklyn. Once I figured out where I was, I began to pace the floor of the front room, stopping at last before the three fist-shaped holes in the wallboard, which I had forbidden all my various subtenants to repair. Much as I have tried to pretend and indeed be otherwise, I treasure both my memory and its symbols, as an injured man may come to prize his wound.

So much the better, I was thinking. A bad night now will give me a better chance to sleep on the plane.

Memory is fully as chimerical as forgetfulness, deceptive as any other work of the imagination, or so I comfort myself by believing. Memory will never serve up an absolute truth, only further examples of the relative. Five, six years went by without a crisis. A chimera herself, Lauren drifted in and out of New York, in and out of my house and Kevin's and the houses of others who are only bit players in the script my memory writes. During that long meanwhile, Kevin and I drifted a little apart, our friendship waning in the manner that passionate friendships between confirmed heterosexuals often do.

I watched Lauren's comings and goings with what I liked to think was benign and paternal amusement. Nevertheless, I organized my life in such a way that I was always free to receive her, when and wherever she might turn up, with her aura of a recurring dream. There came a day which I cannot date, though I remember the hour: late afternoon, near sunset. Lauren slept calmly and I had drawn the sheet up solicitously around her chin. I was going out to buy something for dinner, but for some reason at the door I turned back and looked at her. Perhaps it was some trick of the dying light, its kindness to her face, the dust motes dancing above her in the sunshafts that came through the blind. *I love this woman*, I said to myself, shaping the words silently with my tongue, with surprise and horror, too, for I knew already that I could never trust her.

The next day, appropriately enough, she was gone. I spent the next few years fighting it.

Lauren once told me that I was the only person she completely trusted, and I believe that this was true. The only problem was that she could never stand to be around someone she trusted for very long at a stretch. I believe the subject first came up on the occasion when she made me promise to kill her.

A comparatively recent event, about a year before we married. There were circumstances. Lauren, returning by air from some jaunt to somewhere, came down with a prodigious headache. It went on for days without improvement, until friends of hers, including me, drove her to the doctor, who expressed considerable surprise that she was still alive. Lauren had had a stroke, and for three or four weeks she lay in forced immobility, waiting for an operation that might kill her, or blind her, or turn her into an idiot. It was this last possibility that seemed to frighten her the most.

During the pre-op period I visited her as often as I could, which was almost every evening. It would be tempting to say that I was as terrified as she, but of course I wasn't the one with the scalpel to my head. Even as a pre-op, Lauren was in intensive care, plugged into a fearsome array of machinery. Tiny television screens displayed the most minute movements of her heart and brain, and Lauren wondered, she told me once, if she would get to watch those bouncing balls stop bouncing, supposing things did take a turn for the very worst.

But she didn't often say things like that. For the most part she was a model patient, obsessively cheerful and optimistic. However, there were sometimes moments when she would withdraw completely, turning away from me or whoever, to stare hypnotically at the signals of her life in their regular passage across the nearby screens. Fifteen, twenty minutes might go by like that; then she would resume her conversation at whatever point she had dropped it, so that I would wonder whether she was aware that any time had passed at all.

Kevin was not much in evidence during those days. Hospitals depressed him. He did send flowers, which were considered insufficiently sanitary to be brought into the intensive care unit.

I was not fond of hospitals either, but the worst times for me were those long lacunae in our conversations, when Lauren seemed virtually to stop existing. At such times I was perfectly convinced that she would die, so that our subsequent cheery chatter became as eerie as though she had already become a ghost. Then, the day before the operation, she asked me for a promise. I avoid blind promises when I can, but under the circumstances I agreed.

"I want you to kill me," Lauren said.

"What?" I said. I was too surprised to be appalled.

"If I'm not the same," she said. "If I'm alive and out but not the same." She closed her eyes and went on to suggest a method. There was a long straight staircase in the building where she lived. I could push her down it and her death would appear to be an accident. Lauren opened her eyes and held out her hand to me. We shook like business people on the deal.

Thirty-six hours later we were out of those woods. The operation was a stupendous success, one for the medical journals, and Lauren was neither dead nor blind nor a vegetable. The next time I saw her, her most grave concern was finding some appealing way to cover her shaved head and her scar. She never mentioned our agreement, and in my relief I wondered frivolously if she remembered it, and if not, did that mean she was "not the same"?

Whatever it meant, she never spoke of it again, not even after our marriage, which like the other arrangement was a

39

deal. That came later, when Lauren had exhausted every loophole and wrinkle in immigration policy, and had either to marry or leave the States. The likeliest choice was between me and Kevin, and I don't know whether she asked Kevin first, but I do know he never would have done it. So I became the lucky man, and I've always wondered if it was a matter of sheer convenience or if Lauren did have some personal preference of her own.

Why me; why not Kevin? is a question I can apply to all sorts of situations. A question which came up frequently toward the end of the recurring nightmare I had for some weeks after Lauren's operation, as I watched her, usually with hokey slow-motion effects, pinwheeling down the three flights of stairs from the door of her Tribeca loft. Why me? Why not Kevin? He could have done the job without upsetting his conscience. Though when I woke I usually felt that this last notion was unfair to him.

The dream diminished in frequency and finally stopped altogether, but that night on my couch in Brooklyn I dreamed it one more time. With this difference: once Lauren had rattled and smashed her way to the foot of the stairs and come to a stop against the street door, I was sucked from my own body, translated out of it, as one can be in dreams. Looking back at myself from the new perspective, I saw that it really was Kevin after all. I might have been relieved at that, but Kevin's expression was terrifying. It was not an expression at all. His face was so vacant of memory or intent that it had lost its individuality altogether. The face was caught in the moment of metamorphosis, and I did not want to see what it might next become. The shock of it informed me that I had finally slept, and I rose deliberately toward consciousness, like a breathless diver swimming up toward light and air.

WAKING, I BELIEVED the dream was true, believed Lauren was dead. In fact, I enjoyed the gray comforts of resignation for a good part of the day, before the dream fog lifted and I recalled that she was alive and presumably well and walking around in the same material world as me.

But I had slept, at any rate; I had even overslept. My tenant had got up and gone to work while I was having my nasty dream, leaving me a slightly testy note which inquired how long I might be staying. I cleaned up the dishes in his sink out of contrition and then had a workout and a wash and a shave. By then it was nearly noon and I picked up my bag and started into the city.

There were errands enough to fill a couple of hours. I went to the bank in Chinatown and stood in a line to cash Kevin's check. The computers didn't go down when the teller put it through, which I took as a good sign. I stood in another line to buy traveler's checks for the trip, more of these than I thought I would really need, but then you never know.

After the bank I walked across East Broadway and bought a carton of orange juice and a couple of beef buns. Then I went over to Columbus Park to sit down and eat. Hadn't had a beef bun in many months, and I've always liked the little park. Today the weather was pleasant, sunny but not yet hot, with a light breeze waving the trees and dappling the light on the paving stones. The clientele today was quiet and sedate: some elderly Chinese, a couple of winos stroked out on the benches, and me, eating my beef buns, drinking my juice. Down in the south end of the park three Chinese boys were passing the time by throwing *shuriken* at a wooden door. In the concrete shelter behind me someone had erected a tent and appeared to be living in it.

I wadded up the bakery bag and lit a cigarette. A small white butterfly came and fluttered over the pavement in front of my feet. I pulled *Either/Or* from the side pocket of my bag, not to read it really but to flip through the "Diapsalmata," which is comparatively easy going.

Men's thoughts are thin and flimsy like lace; they are themselves pitiable like the lacemakers. The thoughts of their hearts are too paltry to be sinful. For a worm it might be regarded as a sin to harbor such thoughts, but not for a being made in the image of God.

Thok. A pair of *shuriken* struck a tree several yards to my left. The boys had come up higher in the park. Someone sitting close to the tree remonstrated with them in Chinese. I could see the star-shaped *shuriken* embedded in the tree bark to half the length of their razor points. One of the boys retrieved them and the group moved down the way again. No threat. I looked back into the book.

. . . half the time I sleep, the other half I dream. I never sleep when I dream, for that would be a pity, for sleeping is the highest accomplishment of genius.

This had the unlooked-for effect of making me remember my own dream and I got up and walked out of the park in hopes of getting away from it. I was going south and angling toward Broadway. But to the rhythm of my feet I was hearing the dreary little singsong which begins a few pages later.

If you marry you will regret it; if you do not marry you will also regret it. . . . [repeat]
Hang yourself, you will regret it; do not hang yourself, and you will also regret that. [repeat, repeat]

Several alternatives are suggested in the original score, and almost anything will fit. I arrived on Broadway and continued downtown. At length I came upon an international bank and went into it to exchange some traveler's checks for lire. The noise of the bank muffled the either/or jingle in my mind, and mercifully I had forgotten it by the time I got back on the street. Not far from the bank there was a big chain bookstore and I went in and spent as long as I could manage selecting a new Italian phrase book and dictionary. My old ones had been lost or possibly discarded at some point when I had felt it necessary to lighten my luggage.

Go to Rome, you will regret it . . .

I paid for the books and walked up to Fulton Street. Nothing more to be done, but there was a McAnn's down the block to the east. I went in and sat down at the bar. If I'd ever been in this particular one before I didn't recall it but all of them are much the same: long, dark, and narrow, with moldy paper shamrocks on the walls, thick-brogued bartenders, and serious daytime drinkers. And me. There were black bags under my eyes in the mirror. After a moment of inner conflict I bought a club soda and carried it to the phones in the back.

A few calls of a rather impersonal nature: to the permit board, General Camera and a couple of other rental outfits, even one of the rehab centers. There was a general consensus that some such film as Kevin had described had actually been shot in our fair city. I was somewhat reassured by the corroboration.

. . . do not go, and you will also regret that . . .

It was still early for the airport, but it occurred to me that I could beat rush hour if I started right away. So I went across to the subway stop and got on the A train. It was a long ride and acutely tedious. I had forgotten to get a paper. But I could congratulate myself on saving five dollars on the JFK express. At Rockaway Boulevard I got out and waited for the train to Howard Beach. Then another change for the bus and then the TWA terminal.

I checked in and gave up my bag after taking the books out of it. There were hours left to kill and I exhausted the shops rather quickly. At an Olde English Pub in the terminal I consumed a vile excuse for a London broil and drank a couple of beers, which made me sleepy.

Now there was nothing at all to do but wait. I left the restaurant and parked myself in a leatherette chair near my gate. Muzak and the droning flight announcements hit me like Phenobarbital, and soon I felt much like a switched-off machine, an acceptable state. My flight boarded at twenty to seven. Kevin had booked me a window seat. Sweet of him, I thought. But there was some sort of tower delay and by the time the plane took off it was completely dark.

I turned down the meal and drank midget bottles of bourbon through the dinner service. Afterward I declined the movie also and instead read a bit of the thriller I'd bought the day before, so long ago it seemed. Small-time gangsters were murdering each other in Detroit, very relaxing. In a half hour I closed the book and put out the light. I was nowhere and it was no time and even my personality had been left behind somewhere along the way. Probably it would turn up to meet me in Rome, but by then its character might have changed. A change is as good as a holiday . . .

But I woke up before the flight was over, with a clutching fear that I had lost something. Or rather I had hidden something, and now I couldn't remember where or even what it was. I searched myself and found everything I was supposed to have: addresses, ticket, passport, checks, money. By then there was no chance of sleeping anymore. I ordered a cup of coffee and cracked the blind on my window.

Outside the airplane, the sky was melting into gray. I set my watch ahead to Rome time.

Once, I was very good at hiding things.

The sealed film cans. WARNING EXPOSED FILM OPEN IN DARK ROOM ONLY. Too risky, though, for more than once or twice.

Inside cameras or other items of equipment. Also risky, and only good for a small-volume, high-gain load.

The double suitcase switch. Almost one hundred percent risk free for the carrier. But there's a better than average chance of losing the package.

And later there were other and better schemes. With Kevin as producer and me as head technician. But that had been a long time ago and this trip I had nothing to hide or recover.

So what did I have to be nervous about? Well, maybe it was just that there were about two more hours to Rome and I wasn't going to be able to sleep and there was nothing to do but rattle the bones in the closet. But the skeleton that came strolling out this time wasn't Kevin and it wasn't Lauren. It was Jerry Hansen, who really *was* dead and had been for four years.

Jerry Hansen was twenty-three when I was thirty-five and he had just come out of NYU film school with three or four nice-looking sixteen-millimeter shorts and some impressive abilities as a cameraman and a naïve but consuming desire to become a director. Jerry Hansen got his diploma and walked all over town, dropping off his résumé, much as Kevin and I had done ten or twelve years before. But by the time Jerry got around to it, Kevin had rented a cubbyhole in the West Forties under the name of Chameleon International Filmworks, and this was one of the places Jerry dropped into.

If Jerry's experience was the typical one, his visit to Chameleon would have been the brightest spot in a weary and frustrating day. Because on your first trip, you never get past the receptionist. The receptionist is always a woman and always young and usually gorgeous and she has on a pair of shoes worth more than your annual income, and in the couple of years she's had her job she's brushed off hundreds of star graduates from film school. She tells you the production manager is in California, and you hand her the résumé, and after the first few times you practically run for the door so as not to see what she does with it.

The worst part, in my judgment, is how your feet get terribly blistered and sore. But I have a high tolerance for humiliation, or used to in those days.

Kevin didn't have any receptionist. Chameleon was a one-and-a-half-man operation, if you count my peripheral involvement. Kevin had an answering machine and that was it, so he didn't have any buffer when Jerry Hansen knocked on the door. Also he was between projects and he had quarreled with his last camera crew. Also he liked Jerry, who was a likable guy.

I wasn't working with Kevin so much by then. I had worked my way around to an editor's card and I was happy enough with that. It brought a lot less confusion and slightly better hours and a significantly smaller number of people who could jerk me around. Cutting was mostly an affair between me and the equipment, and I liked it that way. I was married by then, even if we weren't exactly living together, and the security was appealing too. As for the other side of the business, I'd been retired for a couple of years. Not to mention qualms of conscience, the older I got the less I liked the idea of big jail, and the longer you keep doing a thing the more probable it is that someone will find out about it.

But I was still on the board of directors of Chameleon International Filmworks. In point of fact, I *was* the board of directors. And it still felt good to get a camera in my hands from time to time.

I liked Jerry Hansen too, once I met him, a couple of months later, when Kevin had his new thing cooking. He was eager and smart and seemed reliable enough to handle the heavy pressure of an understaffed shoot. There was a touch of avuncular interest on my side too, since he quite reminded me of myself at that age.

So the board of Chameleon International Filmworks approved the hiring of Jerry Hansen as second cameraman, first camera AC, and general "step 'n' fetchit" for the making of a pilot for cable TV. On spec. I won't say anything about the concept except that it was as dumb and pointless as the best of them. The production end was one of those nifty bits of prestidigitation which have brought Kevin a certain amount of success by this time and will probably bring him a lot more before he's done. The actors were getting paid out of profits. Jerry Hansen was getting a little over lunch money, a lot of promises, and a nice new line for his résumé. A couple of students would PA for a credit line. Kevin had the cash for film stock and rentals and the sound man, an old connection of ours who was known only as the Sparrow. You actually wrote out checks to him that said "Sparrow" and nothing else. He was a little odd, but sound men run to peculiar anyway, and he was good and patient and not too expensive and he would work without a boom man if it was in any way possible. I was first cameraman and I was getting paid too, after I explained to Kevin that I was too old and too busy to work for free.

A skeleton crew like that and you love each other or kill each other. And nobody got killed on this shoot, at least not right away. The Sparrow and Kevin and I already could work together with the efficiency of a single organism. Jerry Hansen fit in well, better than might have been expected. He knew what he was doing, but not so well that he couldn't follow directions. He learned fast and he had enormous stamina. So I loved him. We all did.

It certainly wasn't Jerry's fault that the project ran out of money. If anyone was to blame it was Kevin, but you always run out of money anyway, it's rule number one. And Kevin had to take all the heat, which was mainly coming from the actors at first, some of whom were beginning to make union noises, though it was a bit late in the game for that. Kevin used up what was left of his psychological credit convincing them that everything would be okay.

Did I know what was coming? Sure I did. But knowing my reservations on the subject, Kevin talked to Jerry first. I can just imagine how it went.

. . . See, Jerry, this is a very expensive business, you understand that . . . See, Jerry, we got bad cash flow problems right now . . .

Well, Jerry was in for the distance anyway. He needed the picture to get finished. Besides, he loved us too by then. If the basic idea bothered him any I never heard about it. I don't think he did any blushing and shrinking.

I did, though, when Kevin got around to me. And when I found out he was talking about dope I got really disgusted. You move enough dope to make anything and it takes up a lot of room. Which I pointed out to Kevin.

He'd already set up the buy, Kevin told me. Besides, I didn't really have to get involved. Jerry Hansen had already agreed to do the traveling.

Then I got more mad. I didn't think Kevin should be using Jerry for things like that. He was too young. He might choke. Kevin was manipulating him.

He wasn't any younger than we used to be, Kevin suggested. And Kevin would go along to make sure everything went smooth.

So who needed me?

Advice, Kevin told me. I threw him out.

Then Jerry Hansen called me and said that he was working on a special project with Kevin and he wasn't sure about some of the details and Kevin had said that maybe I could help out. Wasn't I pleased with that recommendation? I bit my tongue, however. Jerry was getting into the fun part, being circumspect on the telephone.

In my concerned avuncular mode I asked him if he'd considered other options.

No, he said, he was committed to the picture.

Committed to the picture, Lord God.

I screamed at Kevin for setting me up that way and then we made up and I was in. It wasn't qualitatively different from any of the others, because I was always just the planner. I don't have the nerves to carry. I shiver and shake crossing borders even when I don't have anything, which is always. But I was a good planner and this was one of my better plans and it really should have worked.

Nova Scotia, that was the first point, even though it was halfway around the world from the point of origin. I insisted and since I was the expert who never failed, Kevin finally went along even though it cost more time and trouble. It's always better to pick a point of entry where people aren't overly worried about your kind. Off-loading in Nova Scotia was not going to be much of a problem.

Transport. Jerry Hansen, financed by Kevin, became owner of a sixty-nine Buick with a fresh paint job and a few thousand more miles left in the engine and a lot of wasted space which I redesigned to suit his evil purpose. I drew the pictures and even found a guy in Brooklyn to do the work. Jerry would drive and Kevin would ride and after the bay crossing they would be home free.

We sat down, the three of us, with the maps and the diagrams and so forth, and talked and argued until there seemed to be no uncertainties left. Jerry was alert but he didn't seem overconfident and by the time they left I was reasonably sure that it would be okay. It would have been too, if not for the dogs.

It was ten days or two weeks before I heard anything. They'd gone up fast and got leisurely once they were on the island. The plan had them masquerading as a couple of buddies on a camping trip, and they had the clothes and equipment to play the part. I wasn't in touch because I didn't want to be. Then Jerry Hansen made all the papers by getting himself shot dead while resisting arrest at the stateside end of the crossing.

It was a small item and the story was dead two days later when Kevin showed up at my door. He'd spent most of the interim sitting in the back of a bus, but he didn't much look it. He was clean and shaved and seemed very calm, though I found out later that he'd come to me because he was afraid to go home at first.

"So what the hell happened?" was the first thing I said. Kevin asked for a drink, not very typical. The story by him was simple enough. Everything had happened according to specs until the ferry to Portland. Then, at U.S. Customs there, they turned up with a pack of K-9 dope-sniffing dogs. Kevin didn't know why and I didn't either. The most they could have been looking for were personal-use busts on tourists, nothing like what they got. Oh happy day for the K-9 patrol.

"But what about Jerry?" I said then. "Nobody needs to be dead, a deal like this."

"I know," Kevin said. "He choked. It was like you said. I should have listened to you."

"Choked how?"

"He ran," Kevin said. "He just . . . ran. The dogs pointed and he hopped out of the car and took off. They gave him warning shots and he didn't stop and that was it."

"Why didn't you stop him?"

Well, now. Kevin finished his drink. It turned out that Kevin hadn't been in the car at all. Kevin had boarded the ferry and left it on foot and had not been anywhere near the car on either crossing.

I asked him why that was. Kevin told me that it had just felt like the right thing to do at the time.

"We killed Jerry Hansen," I said.

"He killed himself," Kevin said, and give me a careful look. "Hey," he said. "I feel as bad as you."

We sat there for a minute until Kevin thought it was time to change the subject.

"God," he said. "I'm really in the hot seat now. I borrowed money for this deal, you know."

Kevin was wrong. It wasn't time to change the subject yet. I snatched him out of his seat and pinned him to the wall with my left hand and smashed three holes in the Sheetrock beside his head with my right fist. Cut hell out of my hand and if I'd hit him even once I think it would have killed him. To the credit of his nerve or foolishness, he wasn't overly impressed, though he did go a little pale. I let him go and backed off.

"What's that all about?" Kevin said, brushing off his shoulders.

"Tell me one thing," I said. "On the way over. Did you see any dogs?"

Kevin didn't answer.

"Did you see any dogs on the way over?" I said again. I was having trouble keeping my voice level.

"It's not my fault," Kevin said. "I don't see why you think it's my fault any more than yours." And he never did answer the question. Kevin was never very much for direct lying. He always just sort of omitted things.

That was pretty much the end of me and Kevin. Up until the day before yesterday, that is. I had precious little sympathy for the spot he was in, though events seemed to prove that it really was a tight one. Kevin had borrowed money, and borrowed it from some extremely serious people. Well, at the time I thought I wouldn't be sorry to see him get his kneecaps smashed or his fingers kicked in a drawer, so I didn't offer any help or comfort. But in the end nothing like that happened. Kevin scuttled the picture and bankrupted Chameleon (for that part I had to sign papers) and I don't know what else he may have had to do, but he came through it all without a visible scratch, untouched, so far as I could see, in either body or soul.

I had not touched him either, though in the technical sense I'd come quite close, and four years later I was still uncertain why I had jumped him in the first place. Certainly it had been far and away too late for me to make any useful defense of the innocence of Jerry Hansen. Maybe that was why I'd sheered off and hit the wall instead.

Because I couldn't prove and didn't even really know that Kevin stepped aside *deliberately* to let Jerry Hansen take the fall. That was only a suspicion, a feeling I had. Maybe Kevin had only had a feeling too, that something would go wrong and that it would be serious and that he would do well to step out of its way. That's the same sort of instinct that gets you out of the path of a speeding car, and Kevin had all these reflexes refined and sharpened to a rare degree. And a reflex never stops to worry about bystanders. So it might be beside the point to accuse Kevin of any sort of deliberation at all, or give him credit for it either.

If that was the case, I reflected, sleepless on the plane to Rome, then Kevin was innocent, and could only be called innocent in any transaction he happened to be involved in. Though this innocence of his was simply a vacancy, a vacuum. And the winds which whirled around it could do all sorts of damage to anyone in the near vicinity of Kevin.

We killed Jerry Hansen. With my relentless flair for the morbid, I have often rehearsed the scene. I am confident that Kevin braced him well. Kevin made him feel and trust that fortune would favor him on this business, as it always seemed to favor Kevin's ventures. Kevin would have made Jerry Hansen believe that he was untouchable too.

Then Jerry Hansen would have been so thoroughly convinced of it that he would not have believed in the dogs when they turned up, nor in the police or their guns or their power to harm him. So I can imagine him sliding out of the car and beginning to run, without any sense of genuine danger, in perfect faith that Kevin's luck would save him.

But unfortunately, Kevin had only enough luck to cover himself on that particular day.

Kevin was and remains a very lucky guy, and I have always wondered how fully he was aware of his luck and how much he could control it, if at all. I was wondering about that again when the stewards pulled up all the blinds and startled the drowsy passengers with the sudden light of Italian morning. So I forgot about Kevin and his quirks. Now, with the Rome airport floating up under the wings, if I was going to worry about anyone's luck it would be my own. And for the moment I felt lucky enough, equal to whatever wrinkles and twists might be waiting for me down below, in Rome, and *Come sei bella, Roma*, as the old song runs, *amore mio*.

PART II

"COME SEI BELLA" AND SO FORTH

EVER SINCE AIRLINE PILOTS started to be younger than I am, since they have begun to resemble careless teenage drivers, I have been slightly nervous of flying in airplanes. But what really makes me nervous is the guards in the Rome airport, who really are teenagers, who have nifty berets and sashes and spit-shined boots, and who carry teensy submachine guns, usually at the ready. I stand in the long line for the passport check, my hands already beginning to tremble a bit (though this time I'm innocent), and I think, if one of these guys trips, it's all over.

So I was really very uncomfortable when two of them came and pulled me out of the line. They were polite, but definite, and don't forget the machine guns. They spoke to me in Italian, which I was too flustered to understand.

"Mi dispiace," I said, which means "I displease myself," more or less. *"Non parlo l'italiano bene."*

The guards stopped trying to talk to me. By gesture they indicated that I should walk ahead of them through the checkpoint. Once through, one of them came up beside me and guided me to a small examination room, windowless and empty except for a long metal table and two chairs, one on either side of it. At the invitation of a guard I sat down in one of these, placing my books on the table before me. One of the guards then left the room and the other stood to attention against the wall behind my back. I sat straight, eyes front. Oddly, I felt calmer now.

And I thought I was too old to fit the profile anymore. Well, I suppose it was flattering, in its own weird way.

After five or ten long minutes what I took to be a customs inspector entered the room, shut the door, and sat down in the chair opposite. He was young too, middle-sized, black glossy hair, dark civilian suit, hornrims.

"Good day," he said. His English was precise, mechanical, more correct than my own. "You will please show me your passport."

I complied. He examined the passport without expression, left it open on the table, and looked up at me.

"For what purpose have you come to Rome, Mr. Bateman?"

"I am employed by the QED film company as an editor," I said, helplessly imitating the anglicized formality of the inspector's speech. "I have come to edit a film which was made in New York." In support of this contention I produced a letter on QED stationery which Kevin had given me. The inspector skimmed it and nodded.

"How long will you remain in Rome?"

"One month, perhaps longer," I said. "I cannot say for certain until I have seen the film."

"I see," the inspector said. "You will please show me your money."

I handed over my traveler's checks and he thumbed through them. While he was doing this a guard came in and put my shoulder bag on one end of the table.

"You carry a great deal of money for such a short stay," the inspector remarked.

"One never knows when an emergency may occur," I said. "Besides, Rome has become very expensive, I am told."

"It is true. Rome is expensive. Where will you be staying in Rome?"

"I must speak to the director of the QED film company before I decide the matter," I told him.

"I see. You will please open your suitcase."

I unzipped the bag and the inspector proceeded to unpack it completely. Not an interesting or suspect item in the lot, though, only clothes, toothbrush, razor, phrasebook, the manual. The inspector spread these things across the table and then fingered the lining of the bag. I could not tell if he was disappointed or not.

"You will please empty your pockets," he said, standing up. "Please also remove your shoes."

There wasn't a very good haul from the pockets either. Keys, change, a miniature calculator, date book, lighter, cigarettes, money clip. The inspector squeezed my shoe leather between his thumb and forefinger.

"You will please stand up and lean forward with your hands flat on the table."

Then I received a medium-thorough frisking. He missed a couple of places, but I hadn't held anything back. He finished and I straightened up and looked at him. Now he did seem a little perplexed.

"Excuse me, please, I must telephone," he said. Then he headed for the door, taking my passport with him. In the doorway he paused to say, "You may put on your shoes." While he was gone I did that and also put everything back into my pockets. Ten or fifteen minutes passed before he returned.

"You are expected immediately at QED," he said. "I have taken the liberty to call for you a taxi." He went to the table and began to repack my bag, doing quite a neat job of it, I noticed. When he came to the books he picked up a volume of Kierkegaard and flipped through it with some curiosity.

"You are a student of theology, I see."

"Ethics, really. And in any case I am only an amateur." He shrugged and put the books in the bag, then handed me my passport.

"Your passport has been stamped," he said.

"Thank you," I said. Then the guard behind me said something in Italian which had something to do with money. It might have been "What about the money?" or "Did you find the money?" The inspector snapped at him and he said nothing more.

"Your taxi is waiting, Mr. Bateman," he told me then. He handed me my bag and I slung it on my shoulder.

"I hope that this procedure has not occasioned you too much inconvenience," he said.

"Not at all," I said.

"I trust that you will enjoy your stay in Rome. I hope that your visit will prove both pleasant and profitable both for you and for the QED film company."

"Thank you very much," I said. I might have gone for a handshake too, but my hands had started to shiver again, now that it was over.

The good part about all this was that the cab driver didn't even try to cheat me.

What with all the rush and confusion of this whole operation, I had not noticed or paid any attention to the address of the QED studio, which turned out to be not quite what I had expected. Given Kevin's hints about the budget, I'd assumed the place would be somewhere along the Via Flaminia, or else to the east, in the newer part of the city. But the cab dropped me off on a narrow street just a bit above the Piazza Navona, what looked like a residential block.

But the number agreed with the QED stationery. I hitched up my bag and approached the front door. On the door frame there was a vertical row of bell buttons and beside the top one someone had affixed the QED letterhead, evidently cut from a piece of note paper, with a blob of Scotch tape. I pressed the button several times, but I could not hear it ring inside. After a decent interval I began ringing the other two as well. Making a pay phone call in Rome is no simple matter. You can't use coins, you have to buy a *gettone*, you have to find somewhere to buy it, and then you have to find a phone, which in many cases will not work.

I lacked the energy for any of that, so I stayed where I was, alternately ringing and pounding. Eventually the front door opened a crack and I saw a pair of black eyes glittering in the darkness behind it. A small dry voice spoke to me in Italian.

"*Mi dispiace,*" I said. "*Non parlo l'italiano bene.*" It was one of my more useful phrases. I slipped the QED letter through the crack and it was drawn away. After a moment the voice spoke again.

"*Inglese?*"

"*Americano.*"

"*Triste.*"

There was an insult, if you like. However, the door did open at this point. A small froglike woman stood on the sill, swaddled crown to toe in dusty black. She stepped to one side and beckoned me in. I couldn't recall how to ask which floor so I just started up the stairs.

The QED letterhead appeared again, taped to a door on the fourth floor, the top. I rapped on the door and there was no answer, but the catch slipped and the door creaked open a bit, so I went in. A thirtyish woman was sitting behind a butcher-block table in what looked like a rudimentary kitchen, with a small espresso pot and a cup on the table in front of her.

"Hello," I said. "I am the film editor from New York."

"*Non parlo l'inglese, signore.*"

Terrific. She was dressed like a doll, in a tiny white dress with an enormous red bow at the waist, bows on her shoes, a red bow of lipstick where her mouth must be. She had a sort of flapper haircut, with flat dark bangs chopped level with her eye sockets. After she had spoken she smiled widely, a bright empty smile which suggested that no one was at home behind it. I recalled the business at the airport with some discomfort. She looked like she was doped to the gills.

The smile ended abruptly, like a light bulb burning out. She turned to her left and called.

"Dario?"

No reply. The woman turned back to me, smiled again more briefly, and took a sip from her coffee, leaving a crimson smear on the rim of the cup. I dropped my bag and strolled around the table into the rest of the apartment, a sort of attic space with many alcoves coming off the central area like bones from the spine of a fish. The ceilings were angled and low, and there were skylights here and there. Toward the rear there was a door that looked as if it might go somewhere, and I opened it, resisting an impulse to jump to one side as I did so.

The first thing I noticed was a Steenbeck flatbed against the rear wall, a world-class editing machine, its presence a reassuring sign that someone was actually planning to cut a film in this place. I did wonder how they ever got it in, though; it was about the size of a Volkswagen and far and away bigger than any of the doors. Stacked on the floor around it were reels of film and sixteen-millimeter mag stock, and a couple of empty bins.

There were also two people in the room. A squat frizzy-headed man was operating the flatbed, which I saw he had misthreaded. I also noticed that the image on the screen was negative, which meant that they were playing with original footage and probably scratching it all to hell. The second man lolled on the bed in a tangle of unwound film, which he was busily smearing with fingerprints.

"*Che cazzo fai?*" I screamed, another useful phrase which is an impolite way of asking people what the hell they are doing.

The man on the bed raised himself on an elbow. He seemed

a bit of a dandy: pleated pants, silk shirt, a sort of ascot at his throat.

"We cut zee film now," he said languidly.

"Not like this you don't," I said. I went to the flatbed and unplugged it and ripped the plug off the end of the cord. This got everyone's attention. The man at the flatbed leaned back with his mouth hanging open and the other sat all the way up on the edge of the bed.

"Work print," I said. "Nobody touches anything again until there is a work print. Do you understand?"

It was clear that they did not.

"*Work print*," I screamed. "Goddamn."

I went back into the other room and dug the manual out of my bag. There is a useful section in the back which translates basic terminology into different languages. I found the line with "work print" on it and showed it to the man on the bed.

"*Sí, Sí*," he said, nodding repeatedly. "Yes, yes, yes."

"Well, get on it, then," I said. I was too angry to have any more conversation at this point. I can take almost any amount of personal indignity, but abuse of equipment gets me badly annoyed. So I put the plug from the Steenbeck in my pocket and slammed out the door.

Outside, I stalked along a cobbled street until I reached the river, fulminating silently against Dario, whichever one he was, and against Kevin and the whole enterprise in general. At length I reached the river, near the Ponte Umberto, and I walked a little way out onto the bridge. The water was low and there was a swath of brownish grass along the bank, below the heavy stone wall, which contained the river when the water was high. Looking at the river calmed me and after a little while I merely felt exhausted.

I walked slowly around the bend of the river and then turned back into the city. It occurred to me then that I had left my belongings, practically everything, back in the QED madhouse and film butchery. Moreover, I did not know exactly where I was. Well, it would work out somehow. I finally stumbled into the Piazza Navona and found a seat in a sidewalk café on the eastern edge of it.

It was a bright sunny day and there were many tourists milling among the assorted local hustlers in the piazza. Fatigue from the flight made it difficult for me to think, but my senses seemed abnormally acute and everything looked sharp and clear. Each sound, each sensation, was isolated, as though nothing resembling it had ever happened before.

"The rough cut's a little rough," Kevin had said.

I began to laugh out loud. People sitting nearby looked at me strangely. A waiter stopped by and I attempted to order a beer. What I got in the end was a glass of ice tea, but under the circumstances I thought that was just as well.

WHAT HAPPENED NEXT was that I passed out in the café and slept there for nearly four hours. It was afternoon by the time I woke up, as I could see from the changed color of the light. I was stiff and sore from sleeping in the café folding chair, but my disposition seemed to be considerably more temperate than it had been that morning.

The ice had melted in my tea, but no one had cleared it away. I drank what was left and put some money on the table. Then I picked my way back to the QED studio. This time around it was easier to get in, because someone was waiting for me just inside the door: a smallish dark young man with an anxious expression and a bow tie. He spoke English quite well, if hesitantly.

"Excuse me, you are Mr. Bateman?"

I agreed to that.

"Ah, Dario sends his regrets, ah, his apologies. He wishes to apologize. If he, offended you this morning."

"Please tell him that I apologize too," I said. "The flight was long and I was tired and I lost my temper too easily. Also, I speak Italian very badly and that makes me impatient sometimes."

"Yes, of course," the young man said. He was probably twenty-one or -two, I thought. "Excuse me, I am Mimmo. In future I will translate between you and Dario. I am also to help you with the editing. If you wish it."

"Praise the Lord," I said. I leaned my shoulder into the doorjamb. The cobbles of the street were beginning to float gently up and down like billows on the sea.

"I don't suppose you know where I'm supposed to stay," I said.

"Yes, of course. Excuse me, one moment, I will get the key."

When Mimmo returned I found that I was sitting on the doorstep. I had been dreaming about a field of yellow flowers. Mimmo had my bag with him, I saw.

"Is it far?"

"A walk of half an hour."

"Perhaps a taxi."

I returned to the field of flowers. Mimmo roused me when the cab arrived. I dozed through most of the ride, though I did vaguely register that we had crossed the river. When I next became conscious, I was leaning against a plaster wall. Mimmo was working a key in a huge padlock which was set in a crossbar in front of a green door.

"*Eccola,*" he said, when the lock gave way. He pushed the door open and I stumbled through it. Mimmo reached in and handed me the key.

"At the *trattoria* on the corner they also have a key," he said. "In case yours should be lost."

"Thank you," I said. "Thank you very much." I was leaning against the door, which was open only a crack.

"Tomorrow . . . ," Mimmo said.

His voice faded as I closed the door. It was dim inside, though a window toward the rear let in a little light. There was a large bolt high on the door, which I drew shut.

Underneath the window of the little room there was a bed. Little puffs of dust rose from the spread when I lay down. The petals of the flowers were turning scarlet. I sat up and dragged my bag closer to the bed, so I could hold the handle while I slept. The petals of the flowers were turning blue.

The next time I woke up it was dark outside. I got off the bed and began looking for a light switch, tripping over hard heavy objects that seemed to be scattered all over the floor. Then I found a lamp on a shelf opposite the bed.

It was a small room. There was the bed, with an impression of my body in the dust on the coverlet. On the floor there were a lot of welded metal sculptures. These were what I had been stubbing my toes on, I could see. There was also some welding equipment and a mask in one corner, near the door.

A couple of steps went up into another room. I went in there and found a wall switch. This room was larger and had fluorescent ceiling lights. There were several plain wood tables and some stuffed furniture. Shelves on the walls held more sculptures, smaller ones, and a litter of papers and books, the latter in both French and Italian. One wall was lined with windows which overlooked an enclosed courtyard. Toward the far end of the room there was a refrigerator, a double-burner hotplate, a sink, and a shower stall.

Whoever normally lived in this place didn't look to have been home in a long time. I was sneezing from all the dust. So I took a shower. After I had dried off and dressed again I felt a bit more alert. I started trying to figure out what time it was in America, but that was too complicated.

There was a box of dried pasta in the kitchen area and I boiled this up and ate it plain. It went down better than you might have expected. It had been many hours since I'd eaten.

I cleaned the pot and went back into the front room, where I found a door to the courtyard, which I hadn't noticed before. The courtyard was sizable. There were a couple of ironwork chairs out there and a broken table and some more of the welded sculptures. A wire trellis, about six and a half feet off the ground, covered the entire area. There were vines growing all over the trellis, but they looked more like weeds than grape-vines to me. Still, not bad.

I went back inside to see if there was anything to drink. I found the end of a liter of red wine on a kitchen shelf, but I could smell that it had turned. Never cared much for wine anyway. Since I didn't feel up to going out I decided to forget it. I wandered around the main room fingering the small metal sculptures on the shelves. They didn't seem to be much good to me. But behind one of them I found half a liter of Polish vodka.

Eccola.

I had taken a drink of it before it occurred to me to wonder if it might be metal polish or something like that. But it tasted pretty much like vodka, and it didn't kill me right away. I took the bottle out into the court and sat down on one of the chairs. There was a palish light filtering down through the weeds on the trellis. It might even have been moonlight, could have fooled me. I had another drink or two. Then I corked up the bottle and went back to bed.

In the morning I woke up at a decent hour and went out to the *trattoria* on the corner. With some help from the phrase book I was able to buy some rolls and espresso. Then I spread out my map on the table and started trying to figure out where I was.

It turned out to be Trastevere, the Via del Moro, not far from the river and not far at all from the Ponte Sisto. I saw that it was, as Mimmo had said, a reasonable walk to the QED studio. Well, Trastevere was a good place for me to be, I thought. It might be nice to be on the far side of the river if things at QED were as peculiar as they seemed at first glance.

I paid for my breakfast and left the *trattoria*. The street outside was narrow and cobbled, with low stucco buildings close on either side. I wandered around a bend or two and then I reached the river. A barge was moored to the west bank where I came out, with a cabin on it. The barge flew small

Italian flags. A clothesline ran from the cabin to the mooring post, and a woman was hanging out laundry. I stopped in the middle of the Ponte Sisto and smoked a cigarette, watching her. It was a sunny day, but not yet hot.

On the far side of the river I walked around the north end of the Farnese Palace and then got slightly lost in the tangle of streets behind it. But soon enough I found the Corso Vittorio Emanuele, the area's main drag, from which it was hard to miss the Piazza Navona. From there I had landmarks, and it was reassuring to discover that I could find my way from the piazza to QED without referring to the map.

It was a slightly more structured scene at QED than it had been the day before. The doll-like woman and the frizzy-headed man were no longer in evidence. Mimmo and Dario, who turned out to be the dandy one, were waiting for me, and both seemed eager to please. Dario and I apologized to each other at some length, with Mimmo translating. I managed a couple of politenesses in Italian at this juncture, which seemed to please everyone. Then Dario spoke at even greater length about his aesthetic for the film, et cetera. I think Mimmo edited this heavily in his translation, but it was tiresome all the same. I dozed through it, keeping what I hoped was an expression of interest fixed on my face. Finally Dario finished, inspected his ultrathin fashionite wristwatch, and took off, no doubt to eat a four-hour Roman lunch somewhere.

Mimmo and I looked at each other across that butcher-block table where we'd been sitting.

"You seem like a sane person," I said. "What do you want out of your life in this world?"

"I want to make film," Mimmo said.

"You want to learn to edit?"

"Yes, very much."

"Good. I can teach you to edit. You will learn how to edit. All I want is for you to do what I ask you to do."

"Yes, of course."

"So. Can you find me a screwdriver?"

And Mimmo, with the cooperative spirit which he would consistently display for the next several weeks, did in fact find me a screwdriver. I put the plug back on the Steenbeck. And then we could get to work.

It turned out, not much to my surprise, that we couldn't get a work print processed until the next week. Mimmo, bless him, handled the details of that. I spent one day fooling around with mag stock after the film went out. I was thinking of logging it, but that was hopeless, pointless rather. The original crew had made a merry mess of everything. There were no slates on the sound, though part of it had been recorded with a cable connection to the camera, so there were bloops I could sync up to when the film came back from the lab. On the other hand, a roughly equal part had been recorded with crystal, and for those segments there weren't even any bloops.

Now I knew why they needed an editor who spoke English. I was going to have to sync up half the rushes by lip reading.

Then there was the problem of the sound/picture ratio. There was about ten times as much of the one as the other, or so it seemed to me from a glance at the film before it went out. I asked Mimmo to take up this matter with Dario, since I did not completely trust my own temper yet. What emerged from between the lines of Mimmo's report was the probability that Dario had directed the shoot in name only. The cameraman had run loose and ignored the sound man, who had thus been forced to run miles of tape in order to be sure of covering every shot. After that, I suppose, the sound man would have gone into hiding, lest anyone should call upon him to straighten it all out. *All* of the quarter-inch tape had been transferred to sixteen-millimeter mag. I inherited the little chore of reducing it by a factor of ten before anything which could properly be called editing could begin. I estimated that it would take about two weeks, provided I could teach Mimmo to do some of it for me, to sync everything up. Well, it was their money.

Another strong probability was that Kevin had somehow messed in the nest again, letting a shoot as sloppy as this one go down. The price he'd put on my job didn't seem so outlandish anymore. "The rough cut's a little rough." No kidding.

I bugged out of the QED studio for the remainder of the weekend and turned myself into a tourist. I went to the Colosseum and the Pantheon. I wandered through any number of splendid churches. I took the shortest, most manageable tour of the Vatican collection. And once I was saturated, drenched, with culture and art, I simply walked. I would cross one of the bridges from Trastevere, follow the curve of the river for a gentle shady mile, then double back and find my way home through the twisted streets on the western side. It was a tolerable exercise in geography and map reading and it killed time and tired me out enough to sleep.

I worked over my phrase book some, until I was speaking fairly effective pidgin again. Good enough so I could shop for food to cook in my borrowed or stolen Trastevere pad. And it was a pleasure to cook with fresh pasta, top-grade olive oil, the odd pear-shaped local tomatoes, the variety of available cheeses. A few meals I ate out, favoring the Trastevere restaurants, which were cheaper and less touristy, and finally settling on my own corner *trattoria* as the regular stop.

I let my weekend stretch until Thursday, the day Mimmo thought the work print would probably come in, and I kept clear of QED for the whole time. If I went there with nothing to work on I was afraid I might get irritated again at something or other. So I stayed away. I was exercising and eating well and I was on a fairly strict ice tea diet, except for that windfall bottle of vodka. I rationed that out to myself in small measures, since I'd decided not to get another one. Under the circumstances of my solitude and idleness I didn't want to risk a binge. If my throat itched for an extra drink I'd read a little Kierkegaard.

The vodka ran out on Tuesday and by Wednesday I was beginning to look for loopholes in my austerity program. In the early evening I went to the *trattoria* for an early supper and mainly to get out of the house, and there I remembered about grappa. There's no language difficulty about ordering grappa. You just say "grappa" and the man brings you some, in this case a sizable portion for the equivalent of about thirty U.S. cents. It's not vodka, and it's surely not bourbon, but it's easy to get and not at all bad.

And it was the grappa, the seeds-and-stems burning taste of it, that made me think of the Trevi Fountain, which I'd somehow missed out of my tourist stops. So I left it at the one glass and walked there. It was a long walk and I made it a brisk one and by the time I got there the drink had almost completely worn off.

The sun was going down and it was almost completely gone from the closed piazza which frames the fountain. A single shaft of fading sunlight fell on one of the horses that plunge out of the portico over the falling water. A busload of German tourists stood gabbling around the fountain and I waited until they organized themselves and left for their next stop. Then I went down the stairs and stood at the lip of the basin.

That bar of sunlight twisted farther down, piercing the surface of the pool, and I looked down after it, seeing the flat stones under the water, where all the money lay. I was wondering if my own coins might still be there too. The sun dropped away behind the buildings altogether and it was darker and seemed a little colder at the Trevi Fountain. My trick elbow had begun to throb a bit, as it sometimes does at a change in the weather or a circumstance of stress or an abrupt renascence of memory. It had not been so long ago, not really. But I felt as though I were now standing on the far side of a wall dividing me from my green youth and particularly from another day when I had thrown money into this fountain, to guarantee, according to the old superstition, that I would eventually return to the city of Rome. I had wanted very badly to come back, that day, and I had thrown in several of the nearly worthless coins and even a *gettone* as well. If my memory was accurate, Lauren had done it too.

I SAT ON THE BED in the apartment, under the lighted lamp. On the street outside it was completely dark. I had fallen into the habit of leaving the door open when I was home, as I had little to protect. Outside: the rare buzz of a car or Vespa, sequences of footfalls approaching and retreating, snatches of conversation which I could not understand — the foreign night in its senseless and devouring generality. Within: the infrequent tick of plaster dropping from the walls, dust gathering secretly on every surface, myself hemmed into a circle of lamplight which I believed could show me nothing. A book was open on my knees, but I had no will to turn the page.

"My soul is like the Dead Sea, over which no bird can fly," Kierkegaard writes in one of his more desperately deluded personae. "When it has flown midway, then it sinks down to death and destruction."

There is a lesion between hope and recollection, into which my spirit had slipped, void of intention or desire. My memory was a useless pain, my future a null sign, white nothingness. Could I have willed myself to death without effort I would probably have done so, but I lacked the energy even to lift my hand. In another place and voice Kierkegaard says that it is better to choose despair than to choose nothing. But for the despairing it can be hard to tell the difference, and the despairing more often feel they have been chosen by their state.

I understood that my condition was useless, pointless, and without genuine cause. Only a couple of hours before I had been, if not precisely happy, at least functional, and I knew well enough that in the fullness of time I would be so again, though perversely enough this knowledge was hateful to me now. And how much time? For now each moment had become a miniature eternity of hell, its passage slow indeed.

I was capable of nothing, could move in no direction; even breathing had become a tiresome task. It was pointless even to drink, as I knew from past experience, as I remembered. The best I had to cling to was an obligation. In the morning I would go to the QED studio and cut film; that was my duty.

But I could either go or not go, what would be the difference?

There seemed, distinctly, to be some reason for me to go rather than not go. What was it?

In one way or another I had again become a part of one or another of Kevin's schemes. And I was interested. I wanted to find out what the scheme was and how I figured in it. A rather thin reason for being, perhaps, but it was sufficient to its season.

Now that everything is over, now that my memory and my hope have been in some sense conjoined, I remember almost everything, but I do not remember this black mood. I recall that it happened, of course, but I cannot summon the sensation of it, not that I wish to. When it comes it will come of itself and I trust that I will again survive it, though it will not be Kevin nor any thought of him which gets me out of it next time. But I must give credit where it is due. I owe Kevin the motive that got me off the bed, sleepless or not, wretched or not, and inspired me to work and live through the days that followed. It was neither my love nor my hate that he engaged on this occasion, only my curiosity. But curiosity is itself a form of hope.

Mimmo, poor boy, must have thought that I was mad at everyone again. By the time I arrived at QED on Thursday I was in somewhat better shape than I'd been in the night before. I'd even slept a little, sitting up. I could walk, but I couldn't make conversation yet. It must have seemed fairly grim, and none of it was Mimmo's fault at all. He'd taken delivery of the work print as promised, and somehow managed to make sure that Dario and the others were not around. I knew it was unfair to be mean to him, but I was still too twisted to make nice.

So I didn't try to make nice, didn't even say a word. I walked in, shut down the room light, and threaded the first roll of film on the Steenbeck. Mimmo perched on the edge of a chair next to the flatbed, intent, waiting for me to say something, anything. I watched three, four, five rolls of the film, at speed. Finally my poisoned humor began to disperse, replacing itself with ordinary professional irritation. I began to curse and take the name of the Lord in vain.

"What?" Mimmo said. "I don't understand?"

"Your first lesson," I said. "American swear words. They're very important for editing film."

Mimmo laughed, relieved. And after a moment I found that I was laughing too. And now that I had found my tongue again, I began to explain things.

I explained to Mimmo the whole problem of the sync-up, and told him that what I had been doing for the past several hours was looking for a clue, some vestige of a relationship between the picture and the sound. I hadn't found one yet. But I had found plenty of other things, most of which fell into the category of bad news.

The footage I'd watched was an uneven mix of interviews, shots of what appeared to be rather violent encounter groups of some kind, and scene-setting panoramas and traveling shots with no people in them. There were a lot of locations, and without the sound it was difficult to tell which ones were which. Already there was a problem here, though of rather an abstract nature: not enough action. What I was likely to end up with was a talking-heads documentary. But that wasn't really my problem. You work with what you've got.

From the standpoint of movement, composition, and so forth, a lot of the camera work was pretty good. Some of it I could even admire, if a little grudgingly. Some of it I thought was dreadful.

Scratches, tramlines, and other damage resulting from the mishandling of the original negative seemed to add up to less than I'd feared it might. But there was plenty of other technical trouble.

For instance, screen direction. It was worst with the encounter-group shots. The groups, evidently, had taken place in circles, and the cameraman had wandered around and around these circles like the hands on a clock, completely disregarding the famous imaginary line. Which meant, as I explained to Mimmo, that the close-ups and cutaways were not going to make a great deal of sense. People who are addressing each other would appear to be facing in opposite directions. And so on. A trying situation for the editors, namely him and me.

Then there was the matter of light. Generally speaking there was not enough of it. Film density was poor throughout much of the footage.

Here Mimmo interrupted with an explanation of his own. Dario and his cameraman, who turned out to be the frizzy-headed fellow I'd watched cheerfully ripping his own film to shreds the day I arrived, were both devoted to the concept of "available light." Ah, yes. Mimmo began to elucidate the precedents, but I was already familiar enough with those.

In theory the concept is pleasing, I suggested to Mimmo, but if there is not enough light available to make a legible image on the film, it is better to depart from the theory and add some. Which in some cases the camera crew actually seemed to have done. In other cases, not.

A faster film might have been advisable, I pointed out: 7247 is a very good stock, but slow. Quite slow. Too slow altogether for the sort of light you are apt to find available for your use in dimly lit institutional buildings, night streets, and the like.

Which brought up the point that some of the footage from these darker locations really looked a lot better than circumstances suggested to me that it should. I shut off the flatbed for a moment and inspected some of the original boxes. These boxes had notes on them that said things like "Chemtone push 3" and "Chemtone push 4." It looked like Kevin's handwriting, too. Which indicated a couple of things. Kevin had been on some of the locations. And he had done something right while he was there.

Mimmo was interested and so I explained to him about Chemtone, a relatively new developing process which did several nice things. One thing it did was allow you to shoot under fluorescent light. Fluorescents give a nice hot light, but they tend to have a weird effect on color film. They make flesh tones turn green, et cetera. Chemtone processing can correct for that. It was a godsend for this footage, since so much of it had been shot under institutional fluorescents. The other handy feature of Chemtone was its salutary effect on a push. With Chemtone, you can push three or maybe four stops without getting an overwhelming grain. Without Chemtone, footage pushed that far would look like split-pea soup.

Without Chemtone, I told Mimmo, we would have had to throw away so much of the film that there would have been nothing left to cut. I would have had to go back to New York and give Kevin all his money back, less my expenses. With Chemtone I could stay in Rome and draw my salary, and Mimmo could learn all about synchronization and lighting and developing processes and color temperatures, and eventually he might even learn how to cut film too.

Even with Chemtone there was a lot of suspect footage.

The crew (and shame on Kevin if he had been with them) had operated with a cavalier disregard of the differences between *kinds* of light. They seemed not to know that tungsten does not mix well with daylight, or with fluorescents either, or that when shooting outdoors under the sun it is wise to use a daylight filter, or that when shooting indoors with partial daylight it is advisable to put #85 gels on the windows. Footage with these sorts of problems really ought to end up on the floor. But I could see already that some of it was too important for that. It would just have to go into the final cut and sit there looking peculiar.

I became slightly embarrassed when I saw that Mimmo had begun to take notes. The point was to cut the film, after all, not teach a class about it. I turned back to the flatbed. But Mimmo observed that I had talked my way through lunchtime and maybe dinner too, that it was nighttime now and probably time to knock off. So I said good-bye. Sure enough it was dark when I got down to the street. I walked across the river and had a dish of pasta at the corner *trattoria*. I didn't even think of having a drink or of being miserable. I thought about the film, about tricks I could use to solve some of the problems, about how to get some foothold on the sync situation by the next day. When I got back to the apartment my mind switched off easily and I slept as heavily as a stone.

There was one section of the film that I remembered well enough to go straight to again when I arrived at QED the following day: close-up of a black man, mouth wide open, screaming. On the film, he screamed with what appeared to be tremendous energy, though of course I couldn't hear it. But I could see light reflecting off the fillings in his molars, way in back.

At the beginning of this shot a single frame of film was flashed. It's a feature of Arriflex cameras, to facilitate sync-up when the crew has been too rushed or too careless to do slates.

The Arri flashes one frame of the film and simultaneously sends a tweetering signal, commonly known as the bloop, down the cable to the tape recorder. Match them up, and synchronization is achieved.

All I had to do was find a scream with a bloop at the beginning, on all those hours of tape, and hope that there weren't too many cases of that phenomenon. It only took me half a day to find four such instances. During the search I began to make a rough log of all the mag stock I was listening to. Mimmo, sitting to my left, made a matching log in Italian.

Four chances were enough, I thought, though I hadn't been through the whole batch. I tried the first segment of tape against the picture, but it didn't match. The second one, however, did.

Well, finally. I marked the beginning of the tape with little black crosses, numbered the two strips, and reached for the splicer. *Snap*. Down came the guillotine blade on the mag stock and the film. I pulled both strips out of the flatbed and hung them in the bin.

"So you found it," Mimmo said.

"Sort of," I said. "I found thirty seconds out of a lot of hours. But it's a start."

And it was a good start too, if not exactly a fast one. I was oriented now. I could tell which hour of tape was apt to correspond with which five minutes of film. And the needle-in-the-haystack quality of the whole enterprise was greatly diminished thereby.

We broke for a fast lunch (none of your two-hour extravaganzas with a lengthy nap attached) and then came back to the flatbed. The work began to go a little quicker. I was able to match up six or seven different takes in the vicinity of that useful scream. At four-thirty I quit looking for more and began splicing the synchronized takes together — chop and tape, chop and tape, my hands picking up speed as the disused reflexes returned. Halfway through, I switched chairs with

Mimmo and guided him while he finished. Then I showed him how to roll the spliced film onto a core. We put the reel on a separate shelf, to go out for coding later. By then it was five-thirty and it had been a good enough day's work for me.

Mimmo caught on to the game so quickly that after a couple of days, for efficiency's sake, I put him on a swing shift. I arrived daily in the early morning and worked on the sync-up till noon, concentrating on the more difficult segments which required lip reading. Mimmo would show up for lunch and in the afternoon he sat by the flatbed, translating my log into Italian for Dario's eventual edification and picking up such tips as I could throw his way. At five-thirty or six I would knock off and Mimmo would move over to the flatbed, to work through the evening on the bloop-and-flash segments, which were a little easier to figure out. I don't know how late he was working, but he always had a decent amount to show for the time by the next day.

The general atmosphere at QED remained benign. Dario was dropping in occasionally in the afternoons. That worried me a little, since I didn't require any directorial interference from him at this stage. But Mimmo persuaded him to stay clear of the editing room, at least while I was there, pointing out, I assumed, that the real cutting would not begin before the sync-up was complete.

The doll-like woman, who went by the name of Carmen, was also there a good part of each day. Mimmo explained to me that she was serving as a sort of general secretary for the project. She was also the liaison between Dario and RAI, the network which would eventually broadcast the film, or so everyone seemed to hope. Fey as she seemed, Mimmo told me, she was well wired into the film circle of Rome, which tended to be, as I knew from previous visits, quite tight and incestuous. When she was present, she handled the phone. When she was gone, it did not seem to ring, which suited me perfectly well.

Dario's fuzzy-headed cameraman, Grushko by name or alias, did not turn up again. Mimmo was even more relieved at that than I. Mimmo did not get along with Grushko personally, and he was doubtful of his technical competence (a suspicion which was borne out by some but not all of the footage). Grushko could be difficult to work with, Mimmo said. He was highly temperamental and spoke neither Italian nor English. But he was not likely to trouble us any time soon. His Italian visa had apparently run out, and Mimmo thought that he had probably returned to Bulgaria, his native land.

The ownership of the QED apartment remained unclear to me. Both Carmen and Dario sometimes spent the night. Mimmo, I think, also crashed there from time to time. There was a regular flow of other guests who passed through for a day or two. It made no difference to me so long as they all stayed out of the cutting room, which they seemed to do. Sometimes, as I left in the evening, a sort of dinner party would be under way. On Carmen's invitation, I hung around for one of these, but the effort to speak and understand soon gave me a headache, and the old man who ran the *trattoria* near my place was a better cook than Carmen. Carmen's acquaintances seemed to belong to some sub-glitter set of Rome, and they didn't interest me very much. Several of them might be taking something, I suspected, like Carmen often seemed to be, but none of them showed any tracks, and there was no trace of works in the bathroom I could see.

I was busy enough that I didn't require any social life anyway. I liked the relative solitude of the editing room, dark except for the light behind the screen and a small bulb over the plates and the splicer. Everything within that small orb of light was completely under my control. The flatbed was ultimately reliable; I knew that it would only put out what I put into it. The rhythm of the work sustained me, and at the end of each day I was calm.

The evenings were still cool and crisp, though the days were getting hotter, and I began to look forward to the slow walk across the river. Each night I'd stop into the *trattoria* for a meal or at least a glass of grappa. The owner, Signor Strozzi, knew me now, since I was turning up most days for breakfast and dinner too. I liked the regularity of it, and Strozzi was nearly as reliable as a machine himself. After a very few days I felt completely enwombed in my new habits. Nightly, I'd find Strozzi at the same position behind his counter, a white apron covering his street clothes, gray hair feathering around his head. I'd drink or eat something, whichever, and we'd exchange some phrase book courtesies about the weather or the food. Back home (it did begin to seem like home), no thought distracted me from sleeping. I'd lie on my back in the narrow bed, and let the day repeat itself within its ordered limits: the regular snapping of the splicer, the hiss of film over the sprockets, the frames gliding smoothly across the screen, one image evenly succeeded by the next.

Thanks to Mimmo's working nights, we finished the sync-up by the afternoon of the twelfth day. It had gone a bit quicker than I'd thought likely, and I was pleased with that. We'd worked straight through one weekend, and I noticed for the first time that there were black rings around Mimmo's eyes. He'd been working a little beyond himself probably, and not telling me. I decided it was time to take a couple of days off before we started trying to put a rough cut together. The last few rolls still had to be coded anyway.

I packed Mimmo off for home or wherever he wanted to go, and spent an hour cleaning up the cutting room. It was still dreadfully early when I left QED, however, and on the walk home I began to feel slight prickles of anxiety, began to wonder if the free time I'd awarded myself would throw me back on the ropes again. I was a little nervous of shutting myself into the apartment right away. So I stopped off at the *trattoria* for a premature drink.

As it happened, I was the only one in the place at that early hour. I sat at the counter and ordered my usual tumbler of grappa. Setting the glass before me, Strozzi remarked that I was in earlier than usual.

"È vero," I said. I resorted to the phrase book for a crude approximation of "The work finished early today."

Strozzi said something I didn't catch. I shrugged, as I usually did when that happened, and drank off half my grappa, feeling the warmth of it spread through my trunk. Then Strozzi's line finally registered in my brain.

"La sua sposa è ritornata."

"La mia sposa?" I said. I was slightly taken aback, though I assumed that I'd probably just misunderstood.

"Sì, sì," Strozzi said, smiling. I must have looked bemused, for he began to pantomime. He jerked his thumb in the direction of my apartment, made a motion with his thumb and forefinger as if turning a key, and nodded vigorously several times.

Of course, I didn't believe it. Probably what had happened was that the rightful owner of the apartment had reappeared, or that Dario or Carmen might have seen fit to furnish me with a roommate.

But the possibility, however faint, however ludicrous, was interesting. It was almost a physical sensation, tingling in my chest. I finished the grappa, but stayed there on my stool. For some reason I didn't want to think in English. I repeated Strozzi's words to myself, la sua sposa, then switched to French, which I understood a little better: mon épouse, ma femme, mon amour. I swung on my stool toward the open door and looked at the sunlight on the cobbles there, tasting the foreign words as they formed in my mouth, remembering love with its language.

THERE WAS A burning smell when I opened the door of the apartment, and that frightened me unreasonably, beyond the merits of the situation. I felt as though the building were on fire, but it turned out only to be a pan on the hotplate. Evidently someone had started to cook and then forgotten or abandoned the project. I turned the heat off and opened a window to let the smoke out. The scorched pot contained what had perhaps been meant for a tomato sauce. From habit I scraped up the burn from the bottom and stirred it into the mixture.

A curl of smoke hovered along the ceiling and twisted down to pass through the door of the outer room. I followed it. There were two bags near the door which I had not noticed when I first came in; the door swung forward to cover them. One was a medium-sized fabric suitcase with leather trim and the other was a silver Halliburton attaché case of the sort that well-to-do film people sometimes carry equipment in. The Halliburton had combination locks, I observed. Neither bag carried any personal identification. There was a TWA tag on the suitcase, which did not tell me much.

The door to the courtyard was open. Outside on the terrace, my arboretum of weeds, it was shady and cool. Sunlight drifted down through the tangles of vine, tinted green by the leaves, and when the breeze rose the light rippled over the rusted furniture and the cracked cobbles of the yard. I walked back and forth along the far wall of the terrace, smoking, with tendrils of vine brushing my shoulders now and then. There were birds singing regularly somewhere up above the trellis, and otherwise all I could hear was the even breathing of the woman who had fallen asleep in one of the iron chairs.

Another case of jet lag, I imagined. She would have just come off the plane; I could see a corner of her passport edging out of the open purse that rested against her shoe. Her legs were crossed and she slumped a little in the old chair, chin propped on one hand, her long white neck curved a little to one side. She was dressed for fair-weather travel: tan slacks, a cotton shirt, a linen jacket folded across her knees. Her hair had grown a little longer than I remembered it. A thick coil of it hung forward over her shoulder and across the open neck of her blouse, its reddish highlights shimmering in the leaf-filtered sun. I meant to move softly, to leave her undisturbed, but in spite of myself I began to laugh. Lauren had always been a little careless in the kitchen. It was like her to let a boiling saucepan slip her mind.

My laughter was sudden in the quiet of the courtyard; it sounded harsh even to me, and it was enough to rouse Lauren. She shifted in her chair and stretched like a cat. Her long fingers groped for the purse and failed to find it. Her eyes opened, clearing, and she looked at me.

"Will you give me a cigarette?"

"What about 'hello'?" I said. "What about 'I'm sorry I started a fire on the stove'?"

"Did I?" Lauren yawned so widely that her eyes closed altogether. "It's a bloody long trip, you know."

I walked over and set a cigarette in the corner of her mouth.

My hand was an inch from her cheek and I could have touched it if I had wanted to. I struck a match.

"Thanks," Lauren said, centering the cigarette's tip on the flame. "I knew I could count on you."

"You stopped in for a cigarette, did you?" I said. "Where were you coming from?"

"New York. You know I never can sleep on the plane. And I never feel like eating anything until afterwards."

"I know."

Lauren was somewhat frightened of flying, though she had done enough of it, and the long transatlantic hauls could tie her stomach up in knots.

"I was going to make some pasta," she said. "It seems to be what you've got."

"Well, you've made a nice botch of it so far," I said. "I don't think your cooking's improved, anyway."

"Is that a nice thing to say?" Lauren pulled hard on her cigarette. "And it's months since I've seen you, too." She wasn't being arch, she really did seem a little miffed. It came as a surprise to me to find that I still had the least capacity to injure her, however slightly. It was not what I had intended at the moment.

"You must be hungry," I said. "Wait a minute and I'll get something together." I left her on the terrace and walked into the kitchen. The sauce she'd begun was not salvageable, I decided. I threw it out and scraped the pot and put it in the sink. The smoke had cleared from the room, at least. I began to peel an onion and sank the knife into the ball of my thumb. My hands were shaking badly; they went on shaking as I held them under cold water to stop the bleeding. I knew that she would return this way, without any hint or warning, if she returned at all. I would be lying if I said I had not wished for that very thing. But I was not prepared for it.

"Oh, you've cut yourself," Lauren said. I had not heard her coming up behind me over the running water.

"Nothing much," I said. In fact the bleeding had stopped. "I'm getting clumsy in my old age, I suppose." I turned off the water and walked in a wide circle around Lauren, out of the room. In the open door of the courtyard I stopped and lit a cigarette. The cut on my thumb was seeping a little and I licked it.

"Let me see," Lauren said, and took my hand without waiting for an answer.

"It's only a flesh wound," I said. That didn't sound particularly amusing once I had said it. Lauren folded my hand into hers and brought it up under her chin. She bowed her head and rested it on my collarbone.

"You'll get yourself all bloody," I said. "That nice outfit." I flicked my cigarette so hard that the head came off, and I dropped the dead butt over the doorsill.

"You're shaking," Lauren said.

"I know."

"Should I have stayed away?"

I looked down at the part in the center of her hair. *Yes, I might have said, with a fair degree of truth. You should have stayed away. My mind was at ease, and now it is not.*

"No," I said. Though I knew that with Lauren any return was most often only a prelude to another departure. "Of course I'm glad you came." Saying the words, I became so desperately delighted I could scarcely bear it. I raised my free hand and let the fingers of it sink down into her hair.

The bedspread lay crumpled across the sill of the open courtyard door and I found myself looking up across it onto the terrace, again and again. The birds had become bolder; they picked their way among the fallen leaves on the cobbles, coming closer to the door. Our movement on the bed did not seem to disturb them. My body was bending, close to its limit, and each time I felt it near the breaking point I would glance over at the birds and they would spare me for a moment more. From lack of interest as much as lack of opportunity, I had been celibate since Lauren had left me months before, and at first I worried that I might have become awkward or hasty. Not so. At this level, in this act, we had never understood each other so well.

The invisible sun was dropping down behind the rooftops, and fingers of light stroked across the wall beside us, crossing her face, then leaving it in shadow. Outside, a sparrow had reached the sill, and stood at the edge of the bedspread with its head cocked to one side. The bird and I exchanged a glance, which gave me one more instant of detachment. If I was in love again, I was angry too, whether at myself or her I was unsure. It had become a struggle of sorts and I was determined to win it somehow. My hands moved of their own volition, knowing every inch of her flesh and bone as intimately as they knew themselves. I found a grip on the points of her shoulder blades and raised her a little, lighter than air.

"Tell me that you love me," I said. Her face rose up and up toward mine, weightless as a kite.

"I love you," Lauren said, and her eyes closed.

I might have slept a little, I don't know. Lauren was sound asleep when I sat up in bed, and it was almost dark. I dressed quietly and left the apartment, locking the door behind me. My body felt papery, almost transparent, and I even had some difficulty walking. There was not a trace of a thought in my head. I walked for some distance before I found an open market, where I bought bread and cheese, a pack of cigarettes and a bottle of wine. When I came back the bed was empty and Lauren was gone.

Of course I panicked, for in a way I had expected something of the sort to happen. The pattern was familiar. I stood in the doorway for a moment, near paralysis, and finally noticed that the two bags were still there. That at least proved that the whole episode had not been a dream. Then I heard water running toward the rear. I went into the main room and Lauren was in the shower. My relief was so overwhelming it was almost insane. I reached into the shower to embrace her and got myself soaking wet. Lauren began to laugh, and I was giddy too.

When Lauren was with me I often suspected that perhaps I might have imagined her, that she was a fantasy, an anima projection. But as long as I was with her, it was the rest of the world that seemed like a dream. I don't recall now exactly how the next couple of days were passed. We spent a great deal of time in bed, we ate a lot, and we walked in the city. I was drinking hardly at all, forgoing even my evening glass of grappa in deference to Lauren and her return. I did introduce her to Signor Strozzi, and with her superior Italian she soon knew him better than I did. I don't think we talked a great deal, and certainly of nothing of importance. Past and future were excluded from our conversation, as if by mutual agreement.

At the end of the two days I had to emerge from this concupiscent cloud and go back to work at QED. Lauren was left to her own devices. I promised to get her a spare key from Mimmo; meanwhile she could use the one ordinarily kept by Strozzi. Of course it occurred to me, that first day back on the flatbed, and other days afterward, that I might return to find the door locked, the bags gone, and no sign left to indicate that Lauren had ever been anything more than a ghost summoned up from the more shadowed regions of my mind. But at the close of each day I found that that had not happened after all, and by the end of the week my anxiety on the subject began to fade.

There was enough work to fill up my days to the brim and prevent me from worrying about much of anything else. In the first place, Dario's interest in the proceedings flared up again once the sync-up and the coding were complete. He began to hang around the editing room, and his presence made me nervous. What Dario wanted from me was a version of the impossible: he wanted his film turned into a great work of art. I wasted much time during the first week of the rough cut listening to Mimmo's translations of Dario's most ponderous ideas, many of which were either not really translatable or senseless in the first instance. I counterattacked with barrages of technical information which I suspected that he in his turn would have trouble understanding. Under ordinary circumstances, I would have lost this little game, but since I was getting paid through an outside channel I could deal from a position of strength. Also, Mimmo aided and abetted me in the project to detoxify Dario. Together, during that first week, we prevailed upon him to accept what could be accomplished, rather than merely wished for. By the week's end his visits to the cutting room had become infrequent and perfunctory, and Mimmo and I were getting more done.

Once I got used to the limitations, it wasn't a particularly difficult cutting job. There was no question of being artistic; the material simply was not there. All I had to do was turn out reasonably solid craftsmanship. It was journeyman's work, but I've never objected to that. Along about the end of the second week I knew the film could be cut into a decent piece of television — not extraordinarily good, not exceptionally bad.

In a few days' work with the logs, Mimmo and I put together a loose overall structure for the program, like the outer edges of a puzzle. After that was done it was mainly a matter of filling in the pieces. And at this point the work became less fully absorbing. Fortunately or unfortunately, it allowed my mind to wander.

I fell into the rhythm of working by rote, and the job began to go faster. Pieces fell into their appropriate places: establishing shot, interview with some rehab center official (here endless match cutting was required, to create an illusion of continuity where in truth there was none), cutaway to encounter group, some horror story told by a client, cutaway to a street scene, say, and then another horror story. This assembly of parts was satisfactory, yet my mind drifted. I began to feel a vague unease, to suspect that certain pieces missing from the puzzle would never be found or had never been there at all. There were many horror stories from the clients, the recovering addicts. They addressed me more and more insistently from the Steenbeck's screen, that cube of light in the darkened room, and in my mind I mumbled vague excuses: *But we were never in the hard stuff anyway . . . well, cocaine sometimes . . . well, a lot maybe, but that's for the rich, the privileged, the safe, not for you, street junkie . . .*

And I wondered if Kevin might have had such defensive thoughts as these when he filmed these people and recorded their words. I was quite certain that he had not. But the question remained, another missing piece, a fragment that hadn't been developed on the film.

With this background speculation about Kevin came other, unrelated concerns about Lauren. The plates on the Steenbeck whirled; I went on cutting and splicing, and yet as the completed segments of the rough cut rolled back behind me, the questions which I would not ask directly, the big ones and the little ones, kept coming back again and again. A big question: Why had she come back to me, and did she intend to stay this time? A small one: Why had she completely unpacked the cloth suitcase into the shelves of the apartment and left the Halliburton, which one would have expected to contain the most crucial articles, locked shut in the same place on the floor near the entrance where I had seen it that first day? I told myself the questions didn't matter. That it was only my editorial habits, the training of the cutting room, which made me want to force all inconsistent information into some sort of conformity. The theory was reasonable and rational, but as time went by I believed it less and less.

The questions (they had hardly matured into suspicions) only troubled me during the workday, when I was apart from Lauren. Together, we were both completely absorbed in the bewilderment of our passion, which as I knew from repeated experience only grew stronger over the course of her disappearances and returns. I knew that one way or another it was her very elusiveness which gave her such a hold over me when she was there. Of course I also understood that she might also exercise that influence over others, and most probably did so. Whether she was aware of how and why she did it I was unable to guess.

And when I was with her, I truly did not care, for she did make me happy. It is a quality of such love as this to make ordinary actions and objects glow, suffused in an aura of the heart's delight. At our best moments together, Lauren and I had always been able to take possession of this joy. What we had failed with an equal consistency to do was to transform the delirium into contentment, to endure the dailiness of a mutual life. I could and did remind myself that this failure characterized by far the greater part of our marriage, if you wanted to call it that. But during the good times, I loved Lauren for her mystery, her impenetrability, as much as for anything else. Much of what Kierkegaard says about women is wrong or at least cannot travel across the century. But often I think he was right to believe that the mystery of woman cannot be reduced and that it is an error, a dangerous one, to try. Though sometimes the impulse is irresistible.

Then it was June, almost the end of June, and Lauren had been in Rome for over a month, and I was done with the cut. I had come as close to making a silk purse out of that sow's ear as I believed anyone could have done, and now there was nothing left to the job but the tedious chore of A and B rolling the original footage. There hadn't been a peep out of Kevin the whole time, but that was typical Kevin. I was my own boss if you discounted Dario, who seemed easy enough to discount. I decided that Mimmo and I deserved another short holiday before we got into the final phase.

On the afternoon of my vacation day, Lauren and I met by prearrangement in the Piazza del Popolo, and had an ice and an espresso in a bar there. Afterward we climbed the staircase at the western end of the square to the smaller and seedier Piazzale Napoleone, whose eminence overlooks the river and the western end of the city. We had not been talkative. Lauren seated herself on the gray stone balustrade and looked out over the western rooftops into the beginning of sunset. I paced a little away from her, smoking, and then returned to take her hand. She had lovely hands, long, elegant, tapered, the hands of a Flemish Madonna. I spread her fingers, bending them a little, and traced the lines of her palm.

"What do you see?" Lauren said. "In my future."

"I see a fair man and a dark man," I said. "A long journey over water. Much trial and tribulation, to be followed by success and happiness." I was joking, but the words made me sad as I spoke them and I dropped her hand. The falling sun made me squint a little as I looked out over the river at the silhouette of Saint Peter's, which dominated the horizon. It occurred to me with a minor pang how similar this setting was to that of our first meeting in Florence.

"A little more specific, please," Lauren said lightly. I lifted her hand but did not look at it.

"I see trouble and darkness," I said, mimicking some generic foreign accent. "I feel that the lady suffers from uncertainty of mind. Difficult choices lie ahead and she may find it difficult to choose."

Lauren nudged me in the ribs.

"Don't make it so gloomy," she said. "Isn't there a happy ending out there somewhere?"

"*Signora*, I am unable to see that far." The truth was that I suddenly did feel very despondent. I turned away from her and leaned back against her lap.

"What are you doing here, anyway?" I said. There, it was finally out, making sound in the air. "Why did you come to Rome this time?"

Lauren put her hands around my head and covered up my eyes.

"Is it really so important?" she whispered in my ear. "Do you really have to know?"

"I'm going into one of my rational phases, I'm afraid."

"Don't do that."

"Can't help it, you know, sometimes."

Lauren took her hands away.

"I wanted to be with you again," she said. "Couldn't that be enough?"

"If I believe it," I said. Once I get started it's often hard to stop. "Sorry, slipped out. I believe it."

"You ought to believe it."

"I don't suppose it would be possible to think of it as a permanent arrangement, then?"

Lauren did not answer, not much to my surprise. I thought again how nothing can be better or at least more manageable than a little.

"Could I?"

"I don't know," she said. I felt her forehead drop into the space between my shoulder blades. "Try not to push."

I turned around to face her, grasped her by the upper arms. "Haven't I been good, though?" I said. "I've been sober and industrious. For a month and a half already. I'm a reformed character, it's written all over my face."

"And now the job's almost over with. Now what?"

"I thought that's what I was asking you."

Lauren lowered her head. "I don't know."

"Same old song," I said. *Come sei bella, Roma* . . . If you stay you will regret it . . . Et cetera. Et cetera.

"All right," Lauren said, looking up. "There was one other reason. I had to see some people here. I could get a part in a feature. A good part. That's how I could afford to come, for one thing."

"Nothing wrong with that," I said. Could this be one of

Kevin's little schemes? was what I was thinking, but there's some limit to how unpleasant I'll be out loud. "Did you see them?"

"I saw them."

"And?"

"Nothing definite, of course. But it looks promising."

"And you got a ticket out of it, at the very least. Well, that's good. Congratulations, if it's not premature. You could have told me, it's good news after all."

"Didn't want to jinx it," Lauren said.

"Oh, girl," I said, and put my arms around her. "You won't jinx it." Lauren nodded against my shoulder. Another line slipped out.

"Why do I get this feeling that there's something you're not telling me."

"Because I can't tell you," Lauren said.

"I think you better tell me," I said. I was right again, lucky me, though not too pleased with the fact. What's wrong with this picture . . .

"Not now," she said. "Not yet."

"Okay," I said, drawing her a little closer. I could feel in my fingertips that she was slightly frightened. "Okay." I was ready to drop the subject, being a little scared of it myself. I thought I might not like the answer if I did get one. I hugged Lauren and rocked her a little, looking over her shoulder into the piazza. It was a run-down little park, not a museum piece like so much else in Rome, and I liked it for that. But now I noticed for the first time since we'd come there that someone had been dropping bloody needles in the weeds along the wall.

It was that night or maybe the night after that Lauren woke us both up, quivering and trembling from some nightmare. In the past she had sometimes been troubled with recurring bad dreams, but if she'd had any since she'd come to Rome I didn't know about it. I tried to get her to tell me what had happened, but she was still half asleep and all she would say was "I'm scared, I'm scared."

So I did something that had worked the few times I'd tried it before. I rolled against her and put my mouth beside her mouth and whispered, "I'm going to suck out the bad dream. I'm going to draw all the evil spirits out of your mind." I breathed against the corner of her mouth and went on saying words to that effect until I could tell from her breathing that she was completely asleep again.

I didn't particularly believe in the evil spirit hypothesis, but I was wakeful for a while after I had performed the exorcism and Lauren was back asleep. I lay on my side with my eyes open and stared at the corners of the room. The locked silver case by the door seemed to have some sort of ghostly luminescence . . . I thought for some reason of Lauren in the hospital, those frightening periods of nonbeing that the stroke had given her. There was a flash and a smell of smoke and I felt a bullet enter my left temple, I could even see the parabola the bullet described inside my head, curving over my shrinking brain and exiting through my left ear. My head snapped back, my eyes opened, and it was morning. Lauren slept on quietly by my side, and I wondered if I might have drawn that phantasmal harmless bullet out of her dream after all.

WASN'T GOING TO GO back to sleep and risk having any more dreams like that, so I got up and went in early to QED. Mimmo was sleeping on the floor of the flat and I woke him up and sent him out to buy us a dozen pairs of white cotton gloves which we would wear while handling the original stock. While he was gone I vacuumed the editing room, the floors and walls and even the ceiling, and then went over all the surfaces with a damp sponge. I am fastidious about A and B rolling: no dust, no fingerprints, not even the fog of somebody's breath is allowed to touch my film.

I had the room cleaned to my standards by noon, and when Mimmo came back with the gloves we set up the synchronizer and rewinds and got down to it. A and B rolling is a mindless task which requires little but patience and precision, a great deal of both. To make it a trifle less tedious, I could explain to Mimmo what it was all about. You make two rolls, corresponding to the work print. Roll A carries work print shot one; roll B carries an equivalent length of black leader. Roll B carries work print shot two; roll A, an equivalent length of black leader. And so on. When it's all done the A and B rolls go to the lab and two runs through the optical printer will produce a seamless print with no visible marks of editing, or at least that's what you hope. All three rolls are locked into the synchronizer, and you simply do not make a mistake, as an error of a single frame will spoil the entire sequence.

The A and B rolls are composed of the original footage, to which any damage is irreversible, which is why all the fetishism about dust and gloves and so on. QED's equipment stash didn't run to a hot splicer, so we had to use old-fashioned glue splices: shaving the film at the edges of the frames and sticking them together, which is a nervous-making process, as a slip of the hand can ruin a section of film. But because of my lengthy experience with low budget productions I was fairly fast at doing it.

I worked for a day or so with Mimmo just watching me and sometimes handing me things. In the middle of the week I sat him down in front of the synchronizer and walked him through his own first few splices. He was slow, of course, but that was all to the good; the main thing was that he didn't scratch anything or spill any glue on the film. After four or five days (when I myself was beginning to suffer from eye strain and a sore back) I decided it would be to the benefit of Mimmo's all-round editing experience if I left him to work an afternoon on his own.

That set me free to get out of the stuffy little editing room for the first time that week. I took a walk around the Piazza Navona and then went back to Trastevere. Lauren wasn't home; she was spending her afternoon with the phantom film people who constituted such a simple straight answer to nagging major question A (Why is Lauren in Rome?) that her initial reluctance to tell me about them was left unsatisfactorily explained. The coincidence of her absence and my afternoon off was unplanned, or so I maintained to myself at the time, though in retrospect I perceive that it did have the character of a deliberate accident, perhaps even of deception by omission or some such cloudy moral category. Because nagging major question A still retained in my mind what I already suspected might be a causal connection to nagging minor question B: Why doesn't she ever open the Halliburton — and what's in it, anyway?

My efforts to fox out the combination locks with subtlety didn't come to much, not that I'd really expected them to. But there was such a quantity of metalworking equipment lying around the place that I found I could pop the rivets out of the hasps without making too much of a mess. The gear was there to solder them back in place afterward too, and I even found some silvery polish which covered up the few scratches I left on the finish and made it almost imperceptible that the case had ever been tampered with in the first place.

And once I had my illegitimate peep inside the case, that camouflage job began to seem like the most important thing of all. So much so that I didn't even waste time on a complete inventory of the contents. I just thumbed through a couple of stacks I selected at random and then went to work sealing the case back up again. When the solder had set and the polish was dry, then and not before, I got out my pocket calculator and did the estimation. It was old money, but fairly large bills. My guess put it between two hundred and two hundred fifty thousand, American; what you could casually call a quarter of a million.

There wasn't anything much to drink in the house, so I made myself a nice cup of tea and took it out in the courtyard. Then I paced up and down and let it get cold, because I was excited. There's an indubitable thrill to digging your fingers into a quarter-million dollars of cash money, even when you must assume that it would be unwise and perhaps unsafe, not to mention unethical, to convert it immediately to your own use. But the real kick came from something else, probably the same impulse that led me to become a film editor to start with: the pleasure of discovering the system that can order disparate images and events into a coherent picture. And whether this picture and its ramifications for oneself are pleasant or unpleasant in no way affects the thrill. The revelation of the thing in itself is as intoxicating as almost anything I know.

I remembered the customs man at the airport, his polite confusion at the conclusion of the body search. And now I understood too what the guard had meant with that careless question: *Did you find the money?* In my imagination I reshot the scene of our leavetaking, assigning myself a covert smile and wink to both of those gentlemen. Yes, I finally found the money. *Eccola*. There it is.

What I was going to do about it was altogether a different matter. I could of course have gone to Lauren and asked her something like, Why is it that you're traveling around with a locked briefcase full of a quarter-million dollars, more or less? but that would have entailed a certain amount of embarrassment. I did not particularly want to admit that I had broken into the bag and violated what illusion of trust there was between us, especially since such violations had always been her province in the past. It was pointless and no doubt duplicitous for me not to want to reverse that pattern, but I didn't want to reverse it, all the same.

Which left me in some difficulty about saying anything at all to Lauren. The ordinary topics of daily life had begun to seem rather dry and vacant. To talk on any subject became a strain for me. I took the coward's way out and avoided her, pleading pressure of work. That weekend I took a break from the A and B rolling, took Mimmo into a sound studio for a thirty-six-hour marathon, and completed the whole mix for the picture. By Monday I was back at the synchronizer again, working as blindly as if I were part of the machinery myself. The only difficulty was that at the rate I was going the job would be finished quite soon and I would be deprived of my excuses.

I began to play hooky at both ends of the day, rising early, leaving the apartment before Lauren was fully awake, clocking into QED, where I'd work only an hour or two, then close the editing room and leave. What then? Certainly not back to the apartment, where the presence of the unspoken thing would build until it released itself into some sentence which I wanted neither to speak nor hear. I'd seen the sights and was sick of Rome. My Italian had not improved, but it was still adequate to order a drink in whatever bar or *trattoria* happened to take my fancy. Back to the daytime drinking again, I found it welcoming as a home of sorts. After the second, the third glass of grappa, an odd clarity came over me as I sat wherever, watching whatever was going on around me, which always reduced itself to no more than an abstract dance of lights and shades. It was not oblivion, only an abrogation of my will and conscience, permitting me a flight into a world of pure uncomplicated sensation. Unfortunately I couldn't make it last for more than an hour or so, and then the dullness would set in, dullness which I fed with another and another glass and perhaps a meal if I remembered, until the sun had set and I went back. Arriving at the apartment as late as I could manage, I'd squeeze out a stagnant drop or two of conversation, if Lauren was there, and then I'd sleep.

Lauren, being no fool, could tell that something was the matter, though she didn't bring the subject up. Some nights I found her out when I returned, though always she came back before morning, but more often she was absent while being there, which was worse. If one is to be isolated, it is better to be truly alone. The whole situation reminded me uncomfortably of the last bad weeks in Tennessee before she left. I understood, I thought, that the cycle of her presence was running down again, so that soon it would take her away from me. But wasn't I the cause of it this time? I realized, with some dismay and self-disgust, that perhaps I really wanted her to leave me, only I wanted it to be her fault this time.

The day the film was finally finished, my predicament reached the panic level. There was no place left to hide. I walked a long way around the sweep of the river, under the tall trees on the west bank. When I began to tire I crossed the bridge which runs over the Isola Tiberina and stood looking down at the pretty little church on the island. It gave me no inspiration. At the tip of the island, on the tarmac directly below the bridge, someone had painted pictures of the fish which were to be found in the river, labeling each by name. I stared at the painted fish for a long time, though without particular interest. What I wanted, it occurred to me, was to snap my fingers and be translated back to the country, back home, to doze amid the splendor of the land's decay, content enough with the dog's mute company, but the dog was dead.

"I think we have to talk," Lauren said when I came in, just as if she'd read the writing on the wall inside my mind.

"Sure," I said. I lay down on the bed, sat up and took my shoes off, and then lay back again. "What shall we talk about?"

The door to the courtyard was open and Lauren was standing in it. She was behind me, so that I couldn't see her. What I could see was the Halliburton, which I'd attempted to replace at its exact same angle there beside the door. I shut my eyes.

"Well, what are we going to do? When you're done with the job, I mean."

"The job got done today. Except for a few loose ends."

"What next, then?"

"I was thinking of taking a nap."

That got the reply it deserved. Nothing.

"You're out of character, Lauren," I said. "I thought it was 'seize the day and to hell with tomorrow.' Also, the reference to 'we' is a little confusing."

"I wanted us to be together," Lauren said, her voice shaking a bit, with anger I guessed. "Don't you want to?"

"Does it matter? Yes. Of course I do. But soon enough

you'll want something else more, and you'll be gone. It gets tiresome after a while, you know, for me that is."

"You can't say that to me now," Lauren said. I heard the snap of a match, she was lighting a cigarette. "I haven't done anything to make you say that this time."

"Not yet."

"Well, *what's wrong with you?* It's like living with a zombie. You don't come home, you don't say anything when you do. You're drunk all the time, do you think I don't know?"

"No," I said. "I don't think you don't know."

"You'll *drive* me away, is that what you want?"

"No. I'm sorry. I've just . . . I've got things on my mind."

"Then why don't you tell me about some of them."

"Because you wouldn't like it if I did."

"Try me."

"Okay." I sat up on the bed and turned around. Lauren was smoking, fast and hard, with her free hand tensed on her hip.

"For instance," I said. Here came the difficult part. "What have you got in that briefcase?"

Lauren looked away across the courtyard.

"I can't tell you that."

I got up.

"Why not? Why can't you tell me? We got married. We're one flesh. But you're gone for months at a time and I don't know what you're doing. Now you're here and I don't know what you're doing. And I love you. Dammit —"

I walked over and took the cigarette away from her and threw it into the courtyard, where it rolled and fell apart.

"I love you and I don't even know what's going on with you. That's what's wrong."

I put my hands on her shoulders and she fell into me, pressing me against the door frame. One flesh. For the moment it seemed not an allegory.

"I know," Lauren said. "I know you do." She drew back.

"Okay," I said. "Why can't you tell me what's in the bag?"

"Because I don't know what's in it."

"Well," I said. "Why don't we just open it up and find out?"

"I don't know the combination."

"Terrific," I said. "Would you like to elaborate on that?"

"I'm only carrying it," Lauren said. "Kevin told me —"

"I love this," I said. "I love it already. Kevin?"

"Kevin's making a feature," Lauren said. "It's a good script. I've seen it. Only, well, there were some complications, he said."

I became so dizzy from the shock of sudden comprehension that I had to sit back down on the bed.

"Wait a minute," I said. "Let me guess. Kevin says, 'I'm going to do a feature, I'll make you a star and so forth, only first would you just take this bag full of God knows what and drop it off in Italy for me?' "

That seemed to sting a bit.

"Of course I know it's all some wretched little stunt. You don't suppose I think that bag is full of chocolates, do you?"

"I was beginning to wonder, yes."

"Maybe I just wanted to share all the excitement, had you thought of that?" Lauren pulled out another cigarette so jerkily she broke it. She could be a terror when she was really angry, but then I was really angry too. "And it's not supposed to be Italy anyway —"

"Of course not," I said. "Not Italy. Belgium maybe? Brussels?"

"How did you ever know that?" Lauren said, subsiding.

I could almost taste the tequila again, hearing Kevin's voice repeating as if on a tape loop. *It would be a trip to Brussels if I can work it out.*

"I'm clairvoyant," I said. "Under certain circumstances. Then Kevin says, 'Oh, it could be a little tricky. What about a vacation in Rome to loosen up for it? Don't worry about the expense, baby, this is the big time. You can visit some film people who won't come across with anything except Campari and saltimbocca and maybe a pass at you, and by the way, Tracy's in Rome, maybe you two could get together.' Am I right?"

"Close."

"Then you're here and time is starting to run out and you start to have nightmares and you wake up afraid. Are you afraid?"

"Yes. I am."

"Thank God for that, at least. Lauren, Lauren, how did you ever fall for it?"

"Kevin's my friend. He's also your friend."

"Wrong. Kevin is Kevin's friend. You're better off if you never forget that. Don't you remember Jerry?"

"You know he never felt responsible for that."

"Exactly. When he gets you killed he won't feel responsible for that either. But you'll be just as dead."

"You make it sound so awful."

"I make it sound like what it is."

Lauren came and sat down beside me. I put an arm around her, rubbed her shoulders till she began to relax.

"Look," I said. "Suppose we just walk away from it. Leave the bag right on the floor here. We could go back to the farm. I made enough money this trip to last a while. Would that suit you?"

"Would it suit *you?*"

"Not especially."

"I think I just have to go through with it."

"No."

"What else?"

"Tell me what you're supposed to do. Tell me the whole thing, now."

"There's not much more. I really don't know what's in the bag. I don't know what the combination is. Kevin booked me a ticket from here to Brussels. I have a number to call. That's all. You were pretty close to the rest of it."

"When?"

"Some time next week. There's a ten-day bracket."

"You have a name?"

"No. I'm just supposed to say that Anne Morrison has come to town."

"Then?"

"Somebody comes and gets the bag."

"Okay," I said. "I tell you what. I'll do it."

"No." Lauren stood up. "It's my problem."

"Not anymore."

"Yes, it is."

"You don't know how to handle it."

"Then I have to learn."

"No, you don't. You can't. Look," I said. "It's a miracle you even made it this far. You're not going to make it any further. They have currency regulations in Italy, you know. They open bags and look inside when you cross the border. You're in a lobster trap. Easy in, but not easy out. How are you going to get that bag out of the country? I won't even ask how you got it in."

"I don't know."

"I thought you might not. Look. I've done this kind of thing before. I know what to do about it. I mean, I wasn't counting on anything like it this trip. But basically it's routine for me."

"Then I'll go with you."

"No. You're going home."

"Make me."

"If you insist. Lauren, anything's better than you going any further down this hole. Even if I take that bag to the *carabinieri* and tell them everything I know about it."

"You'd never do that."

"Sure? Go home, Lauren, go back to New York and forget about it. It's safer for you and safer for me. I'll be back myself before you know it if it all works out okay."

"And if it doesn't?"

"Do me a favor. Don't argue. Not about this one. Pretty please?"

Lauren walked to the door and back.

"All right," she said. "All right. I don't believe you'd really turn the bag in, though. But I'll go. Because you asked me to. But one thing."

"What?" I said. Lauren sat down beside me again and kissed me like it was supposed to mean something.

"You'll make sure it does work out. If there's trouble, *you'll* drop it and walk away. Promise me that?"

"I promise," I said, though even at the time I knew it probably wouldn't hold.

The pressure was off for the moment, and I felt that we'd survived something, though exactly what I couldn't have said. We had a pleasant evening after that, out to dinner and out for a walk, an ice at a bar on the way home, and then early to bed — together, for the first time in a while. The morning was a little dreary, but for ordinary reasons.

I took Lauren to the airport, not entirely out of sentiment. I don't like long good-byes. But I did want to be sure that she actually got on the plane. I couldn't be sure how completely she'd bought my blackmailing her into stepping aside and leaving me in charge of the mystery bag. It had never been part of our pattern for me to hand down direct orders like that, so I had my doubts whether she'd be inclined to follow them. And whatever her other faults might have been, I thought a regard for her safety at the expense of my own was unlikely to be among them. While I did have that queasy feeling of being maneuvered neatly through the stages of someone else's plan, it was definitely more my problem than hers, and the first thing I wanted was to get her out of it.

That was the main reason I took the trouble to personally pack her onto the plane. I've never been able to generate much passion in an airport, and in this case I became a little impatient for her flight to be called, partly because I had to keep resisting the impulse to look over my shoulder for that courteous young customs inspector. Lauren felt much the same, I imagine;

she'd always gone in for the cleanest of partings, often with no notice given whatsoever. There wasn't a great deal for us to talk about that hadn't already been said. After a short argument about my own future movements, I finally agreed to check the American Express in Brussels in case she wanted to send me a card. Not that I really expected or wanted to hear anything during the short time I planned on spending there. Lauren would just go home and sit tight, I hoped. I also hoped she'd stay the hell away from Kevin, but her plane began to board before I could decide whether or not to bring it up. One last clutch and a brush of cheeks, and Lauren was gone again.

It was a midday flight, so it was afternoon by the time I got back to the city. I was beginning to feel a little peculiar, retroactively. It had begun to rain sluggishly by the time I got off the bus at Lepanto, but I decided to walk home in spite of that. The distance was greater than I'd guessed it and by the time I got there I was wringing wet. The apartment was cold and dark and seemed shabbier, robbed as it was of her presence. There was nothing to do. Outside on the terrace rainwater dripped miserably from the ceiling of vines. I wished then I had managed to be more demonstrative at the airport. I almost wished I hadn't made her go.

There was no more real business to be done on the film. I'd settled up with Dario, who was reasonably pleased with the cut, so my official obligations were over. But as a hastily conceived excuse for my fading out rather suddenly on the previous day, I'd invited Mimmo for dinner at Strozzi's that night. The crisis with Lauren had made me forget it, and when I remembered I wasn't very enthusiastic about it anymore. I decided to go early to Strozzi's to try to get more in the mood.

Since I was staying through to dinner I took a table instead of a seat at the counter. Strozzi inquired after Lauren when he set up my first glass of grappa. I told him she had left for New York. Strozzi seemed not to approve. *A man and his wife should stay together*, I seem to remember him saying, as he poured my second glass or possibly my third. The euphoria, however, would not come this time. I remember that Strozzi put a bottle on my table to save himself so many trips back and forth from the shelf. I don't remember when Mimmo showed up, or much of anything else at all.

When I woke up I was lying on the bed in the apartment, possessed by that horrible feeling of not knowing how I'd got there nor what I might have done along the way. My shoes were off but my clothes were still on. My mouth felt like a graveyard and my head had turned to stone. I dragged myself into the kitchen and choked down a couple of glasses of water. It didn't seem to have much effect. I attempted to smoke a cigarette but it made me so ill I had to throw it away. My watch said it was nearly noon. I decided I'd best go back to Strozzi's for a hair of the dog and to apologize if that seemed to be necessary.

The *trattoria* looked much the same as always. I could comfort myself with the thought that at least I hadn't wrecked the place, or not beyond short-term repair. Strozzi didn't seem hostile, compassionate rather. I asked him to bring me a coffee and a small grappa if there was any left from last night. He laughed when I said that, which I found encouraging.

I drank the grappa. It made me twitch on the way down, but after a minute my hands stopped shaking. I had sipped away about half of my coffee, and was even beginning to contemplate food, when Mimmo walked in the door, looking a trifle anxious. He took a seat at the counter next to me.

"So sorry," he said. "I mean, I am glad to see that you are well."

"I have a feeling that I should be sorry, if anyone," I said. "How bad was it? Will you have a drink?"

"I think a coffee only," Mimmo said. "It was not so very bad."

"Was it you who got me home? Thanks if you did."

"Yes."

"Dare I ask if I was walking?"

"No," Mimmo said. "Not walking."

"Oh. I hope I wasn't too heavy then."

Mimmo giggled.

"Not so heavy. Signor Strozzi carries your head. I carry your feet."

"Wonderful," I said. "I'm obliged to both of you. Did I do any damage here? Break anything?"

"No. Not really."

"The truth, now."

"Oh," Mimmo said. "A bottle was spilled but nothing more."

"I paid for that, I assume."

"Yes. Everything was paid."

"Well," I said. "I suppose it could have been worse."

"Oh yes," Mimmo said. "It was not so very bad. Only, I was wondering whether you were quite all right."

"Oh you were?" I said. "I was talking, I suppose."

"A little."

"Anything interesting?"

"I think my English is not so good to completely understand you."

"All for the best, I would expect."

"You say many times that you have shot your dog. This is an American expression?"

"No. Completely literal."

"Oh, why then?"

"The dog was sick. Dying. It was a while ago."

"Ah. That will have been sad for you, no?"

"Very sad. I didn't talk about anything else?" A question that was beginning to bother me. It would have been embarrassing to have raved about Lauren. Worse than embarrassing if I'd gone into Lauren and Kevin and the briefcase.

"No. Only the dog, as I remember it."

"That must have been a bit tiresome. I hope you got something to eat at least."

"Oh yes, certainly. The cooking here is very good."

"That's something."

Strozzi brought another round of coffee. I offered Mimmo a cigarette and he accepted.

"I find out this morning," Mimmo said. "I will be interviewed for an editor at RAI."

"Why, that's very good," I said. "Give me a name and address and I'll write a letter for you."

"Thank you," Mimmo said. "You are very kind."

"Not at all. You deserve it. You did a good job on this picture. RAI will be lucky to get you."

"I hope. I have learned very much from you."

"I hope it won't destroy your character."

"Please?" Mimmo said.

"Never mind."

"I must go now," Mimmo said, scribbling something on the back of a cardboard coaster. "It has been a great pleasure. What will you be doing now?"

"I'll be leaving tomorrow, probably. I'll drop the key off here if that's all right."

"Quite fine," Mimmo said. "You will be going back to New York?"

I nodded. Best to be vague on that topic, even with Mimmo. He stood up.

"And you are sure you will be quite all right?"

"Of course," I said. "Don't worry about me."

"Then, *buon viaggio*."

"*Grazie*," I said. "Take care of yourself."

Mimmo went quietly out of the *trattoria*. I signaled to Strozzi for another grappa and turned over the coaster he'd been writing on. He'd left not only the RAI information but also his own telephone number and a note to call if I needed anything. I was touched by that. When I drank the second grappa I felt almost human again, and also I remembered a fragment from the night before. I saw myself crying in the bathroom, staring at myself in the mirror, an ugly sight. Mimmo must have seen the traces of it too, whenever I came out. Well, he was a nice boy. I put the coaster in my pocket. There was no reason for anyone to worry about me. I was set up. Even if I ran out of traveler's checks I still had all the money in the world locked up in that briefcase back at the apartment. And *I* wasn't going to worry about the situation. I was so afraid that someone might find out what I was doing that I didn't even dare think about it myself.

LAUREN

Tracy told me once in some sort of aside that it would make sense if I felt most at home in airplanes. It was meant for a joke, I suppose, but rather a bitter one. I forget the circumstances, but probably he'd had a skinful and probably we'd been fighting. I remember the remark now almost every time I fly, if only because it is so untrue.

I am not afraid, I told myself again, squeezing the arms of the seat as the plane rose out of Rome. I am not afraid of this, reminding myself as always how few planes really crash, how much safer it is to fly than, for instance, to drive an automobile. I believe myself, because I am truly not afraid that the plane may crash. Indeed, I am not even interested in that possibility. That is not at all what matters. What does frighten me is that when the plane levels off above the clouds, finds its location exactly nowhere, then I myself seem also to have disappeared. There is nothing to confirm any sense of my individuality, my borders. I have become a ghost.

After the aneurysm, it became not worse but more distinct. After the operation, once it had been determined that I could still work my arms and legs and organs and senses, the doctors began to wonder if I might be suffering any sort of mental problem.

Why yes, perhaps, but it's really nothing new.

Then for a year or a little less I visited a mental doctor who asked me lots of questions. The therapy would have been called unsuccessful, I dare say. The symptoms, such as they were, did not go away, but I stopped going to the doctor once I discovered that it was no more futile and certainly a great deal cheaper for me to ask the questions of myself. Perhaps I even asked rather better questions; perhaps I was willing to answer them a little more honestly too.

You have said that under certain circumstances — for instance, solitary air or train travel, or other periods of relative isolation — you are troubled by a sense of unreality, of your own nonexistence, as you put it.

Yes. Or rather I feel disbelief in my own immediate past actions. Thoughts and feelings too. My memory seems unreal, not associated with myself. I feel that I have come into possession of someone else's recollections. I also do not believe in my own past or in my future.

You say that these symptoms became worse after your brain aneurysm and the operation which corrected it.

Not worse. Only more definite.

Can you explain?

It seemed to prove that there was really nothing there.

By "it" you mean the preoperative losses of consciousness?

I was not unconscious. I could see and hear.

Then how would you have described your condition?

There is nothing to describe.

Let me change the subject for a moment. You have suggested that you are not entirely happy with the direction which your career has taken. You've been quite successful as a model. A familiar face if not a famous one —

Familiar to others. Not to me.

We'll get back to that. Modeling has begun to bore you, you

now say. You would prefer success as an actress. A serious actress. Do you consider that to be a realistic ambition?

As much as anyone else's hopes of that kind. I have ability and training. I've been told that I have the looks.

Over the past five years you have supported yourself primarily by modeling, and you have appeared in . . . in . . .

Bit parts in a couple of off-Broadway plays, one strong supporting role off-Broadway, bit parts in two Hollywood features.

Yes. Are you pleased or disappointed with that record?

It depends on my mood.

Do you believe in your acting talent? Have faith in it, so to speak?

I do.

Yet belief in your talent seems insufficient to provide you with a consistent sense of self?

Sometimes I wonder whether a "consistent sense of self" would be helpful to my particular ambition.

Let me change the subject. You said previously that your face is familiar to others but not to yourself. What do you see when you look in the mirror or see your photographs in magazines?

A stranger.

A beautiful stranger?

I have never believed in my own beauty.

Circumstantial evidence suggests that others do. Does that outside reinforcement help to convince you that you are beautiful?

Sometimes. Briefly.

Confirmation by others is sometimes meaningful to you, then. Does it generally come from men?

Sometimes women also.

Would you describe yourself as sexually promiscuous?

Not anymore.

But you would have done so at some time in the past?

Up until about four years ago.

That would roughly coincide with your operation. Do you relate the operation to your change in sexual behavior?

No.

You have said that you have had many lovers in the past, and often more than one at a time. At present, by your own account, you are romantically involved, if you'll pardon the expression, with two men. Kevin Carter and Tracy Bateman.

Yes.

Tracy Bateman is a film editor and Kevin Carter is a producer and director. Of the two, which would you say could be more helpful to your career?

Kevin. Possibly Kevin.

You married Tracy Bateman about three and a half years ago?

Yes. That's correct.

It was to some extent a marriage of convenience having to do with your immigration status?

Yes. But I also loved him and wanted to live with him as his wife.

Would he be surprised to hear that?

Probably. It would be difficult for him to believe it completely.

Can you tell me why?

He has an analytical nature and often tends to be suspicious.

Suspicious of you?

Sometimes.

With reason?

Yes. Sometimes.

And Kevin Carter? He and Tracy Batemen were acquainted, is that not correct, prior to your relationship with either?

True. They were very close friends. I sometimes think that they might even have become lovers themselves if either of them had been . . . inclined that way.

But neither was so inclined?

Absolutely not.

Interesting.

Dangerous.

How so? To you?

More to each other. But I have sometimes felt —

Used?

Not exactly. But sometimes that they might be trying to . . . to approach each other through me.

You hesitate on the word "approach." Maybe you mean something else? "Attack"?

Possibly.

There has been some estrangement between them, then.

Yes.

Of what nature?

A general mistrust. On Tracy's side, I should say. Tracy believes that Kevin is too careless of other people's interests and welfare. To the point of ignoring them altogether.

Is his belief justified?

I would prefer to think it is not.

What do you think is Tracy's feeling for Kevin now?

Love and contempt.

And Kevin's for Tracy?

Hatred and fear. No, I would like to retract that. I won't say "hate." I don't know what it is.

But fear, then? Why do you say that?

Kevin doesn't have a logical mind. He acts on impulse and emotion. Tracy knows him well enough that sometimes he can anticipate what Kevin is thinking and even what he will do in the future.

Is there any concrete reason for Kevin to be afraid of that?

Possibly.

Does this situation frighten you?

Yes.

Do you hold yourself responsible for the estrangement between Kevin and Tracy?

No.

Do you think that you have affected their relationship?

Only in a minor way.

You said a moment ago that Kevin hated Tracy, and then you retracted the remark. What did you mean?

It wouldn't really be hate. It's a kind of love with fear in it.

Then there is a love-hate relationship between them.

I don't think that the term explains anything.

How would you explain it, in that case?

I can't.

Do you love Kevin Carter?

Sometimes.

Why?

Often he can make me feel that I really am there.

Why only sometimes?

Because I suspect that the feeling is an illusion.

Do you think that he loves you?

I don't know. Not all the time. I said he was impulsive.

Your marriage to Tracy Bateman has not been a great success.

No. Not really. He blames me for that.

Do you blame yourself?

No. Though my . . . my withdrawals were part of the problem.

By "withdrawals" you mean your sense of not really existing.

Yes. But he does it too. Something similar. Usually when he's drinking.

His abuse of alcohol disturbs you?

Yes. Very much.

Why?

He disappears inside it.

Do you think that he loves you?

I know that he does.

Do you love him?

Yes.

Why don't you stay with him?

I don't know.

Does he also make you feel that you are, as you put it, "really there"?

He makes me feel that I ought to be.

Do you relate your sense of nonexistence with his withdrawals?

In a sense.

In what sense?

I fear that it is the condition of all human life.

Let me change the subject. You have said that sometimes you are troubled by very severe nightmares.

Yes.

Recently?

Yes.

Can you explain them?

Not really.

Try.

I feel that there is someone inside of me trying to talk to me. Maybe it wants to get out.

Do you associate your nightmares with your occasional sense of nonexistence?

Yes.

Recently, have these feelings of nonexistence got better or worse?

They've changed.

In what way?

I have realized that I am no longer only my own life but something else too.

That's rather cryptic. Could you elaborate?

I'd prefer not to. At least not now.

Is this new sensation related to your nightmares? The idea that something inside of you wants to get out?

Not at all. It's much more concrete.

And when did you first become aware of it?

Gradually. But I became certain of it today. On this airplane.

What do you plan to do about it?

I haven't the slightest idea.

PART III / CHOC EN RETOUR

ETWEEN July 11 and July 13, the accused (Tracy Bateman, a United States citizen) traveled in the north of Italy, ostensibly for the purpose of tourism, using as transport a rented automobile. On the morning of July 14 (Bastille Day — how do you like that?) he crossed the French-Italian border, again ostensibly for the purpose of tourism, but with a covert intention to . . ."

To what? Even I didn't know the answer to that one, though I was assuming it would all become clear in due course. But it did while away the time, when I was doing all that driving, to make up different police or prosecutors' reports about my activities. The problem was that they were all rather inconclusive. Could I be guilty of committing a crime without knowing what it was? You bet I could.

My big hope was that if I did get nailed it would be in a country where the judges and lawyers still wear wigs.

Well. I hadn't been far behind Mimmo, getting out of Strozzi's. I went back to the apartment, drank some more water and two raw eggs, and slept for about twelve hours. In the morning I was fit to face the world again. Not knowing when

I'd have another such convenient opportunity, I spent an hour doing some more tricks with the metalworking equipage. There was a creaky old manual typewriter in the apartment and I typed a couple of address labels and then went out to mail a package. There was a minor hassle about postage, because the mail clerk and I didn't understand each other too well, but no problem over the customs declaration. "Books and papers." No insurance required. I went back to the apartment.

As always seems to happen, my gear had swelled or something during the time I'd spent in Rome. But I finally managed to get it all shut in the shoulder bag somehow. I went over to Strozzi's to drop off the key, and drank a cappuccino while he called me a taxi.

Another minor hassle, over the fare at the airport. I argued and beat the man down a little. It's expected; you're noticed if you don't. Inside the airport I went to the car rental desk, where they spoke English. I negotiated a one-way rental on a four-seater Renault and tore off a rather thick sheaf of traveler's checks, to pay half in advance. There was no hitch. The teenagers with the Uzis didn't seem to be interested in me today. It took only ten minutes for the car to be delivered to the front of the building. The little Renault was clean and still smelled new. I threw my bags on the passenger seat and drove away.

L'autostrada del sole. Superhighways are truly all the same. This one, the road to the north, was flat and straight as a string. The countryside it went through was quite without interest. The monotony of the road was enough to depersonalize even Italian drivers, no mean achievement, that. I might as well have been driving through Kansas.

Around what some people would call tea time, I arrived at Siena, and parked the car outside the city wall. Buses, many of them with German plates, were disgorging thousands of tourists in the same area. I merged with this crowd walking into town, and near the square I broke away. It took me several failed attempts before I found a *pensione* with a room free for the night. I left my bags in the room and walked out around the sweep of the tilted square. The piazza was full of pigeons and people who seemed to be hippies of a kind. I climbed the campanile and looked down on the fan of yellow flagstones from above. Then I came down and had an early supper. A couple of local papers that I'd bought to try to read in my room quickly put me to sleep.

I'd done my work and now I was on vacation. I looked like a tourist. I even *felt* like a tourist.

Early in the morning, I was on the *autostrada* again. I wasn't paying much attention to where I was going. The drone of the road kept me reasonably tranquil. I would put my mind to selecting a nice border crossing when I got farther north. But when I saw the road sign for Firenze I had to pull off the road for a moment to think.

The thing was so obvious, and especially in view of recent events, it was hard to believe that I could have forgotten it. Lauren had been in Florence with Kevin. I had the people, the place, and even a rough date, all thanks to Harvey's super-8 film. April. *Sync it up.* Kevin had let me assume that Lauren had been in New York. Lauren had let me think much the same thing. But chances were she'd been in Italy all along. Terrific, but what did it mean? I ran Harvey's film back across my mental shadow box, as well as I could remember it. The Halliburton hadn't been in the shot, had it? I looked at the thing, lying there in the passenger seat next to the bag I'd started out with. Ordinarily, you wouldn't take something like that on a sightseeing excursion anyway. Though everyone did seem to be terribly casual about this deal, whatever it might turn out to be.

How would I like to cut that scene? I'd like to cut it out, is what. I decided against going to Florence, and took the road west toward the Mediterranean coast, where I remembered, among other things, that the border posts were agreeably casual.

I made good time along the western road and got off it as soon as I was near the water. The *autostrada* had begun to get to me. I found a winding coastal secondary road and continued north, more slowly. There was an almost uninterrupted chain of little resort towns on the west side of the road, but there was not much traffic. At many bends of the road I could see the ocean. Among the older buildings along the beach, there were a lot of modern high-rise-style hotels. A few miles short of Ventimiglia, I checked into one of these.

The hotel seemed to be nearly empty, but for some reason they gave me a room on the sixth floor. It was an American-type single, much like what you'd find at any Holiday Inn, but there was a small balcony overlooking the sea. I dropped my bags, opened the glass doors to the balcony to air the room, and went out to walk on the pink cement promenade which ran along a shelf above the beach. There were palms along the walk. I saw few other people. The sand below was a startling white, and sea and sky were different fantastic shades of blue. I walked about a mile past more hotels and shops and came into a little town built in terraces down toward the waterline. Halfway down a flight of stairs to the shore I found a seafood restaurant which proved quite good, though overpriced. I ate alone on the porch in the twilight, and it was dark by the time I paid and left. I bought a bottle of Campari and some *acqua minerale* on the way back to the hotel.

A sliver of moon hung above the balcony. There were not many lights along the shore. I could just see the white foam of the surf lapping against a stone breakwater around a curve of the beach to the south. Except for the water it was utterly quiet. I could have stayed there happily for a week or a month, but unluckily I seemed to have deadlines to meet.

Kevin. Kevin and Lauren and me. Well, I had cut Lauren out of the picture, or hoped that I had. Kevin and me and persons unknown. "Anne Morrison's" friends, or enemies, or whatever.

My natural impulse was to attack the situation with logic, and logic turned it into a simple conspiracy, albeit with some quite elegant manipulations involved. Assuming complete premeditation, the scenario ran like this: Kevin had cooked up a proposition for me whose main function was only to position me in Rome. That went a long way toward explaining why he'd offered me twice what the edit was really worth. With the fellowship of thieves and schemers, I could now properly appreciate the fact that he'd only paid me half up front. My bet was that the other half, supposing I ever saw any of it, would be called my cut of whatever the deal turned out to be, and considering the size of the initial investment, he'd probably be getting my services pretty cheap. For stage one, then, all points go to Kevin.

Stage two: Kevin seduces Lauren with a script and some fluff about the mythical feature, or if he happened to catch her in one of her periodic spells of ennui, a promise of activity of any kind might have done the trick. By whatever means, he props her up with the suitcase full of cash and a set of instructions and then gives her a little nudge my way.

If Kevin understood me as well as I understand him, he could have predicted what was going to happen next. He could anticipate that I would worm Lauren's mission out of her before I let her get away. That once I knew, I would chew her out and send her home and take over the job myself. Then it wouldn't matter a bit that Lauren was not completely up to doing it herself, that she would have been either shot or arrested the second or third move she made. (Though I did intend to have a conversation with Kevin about those kinds of possibilities if and when I ever made it back to the States.)

If Kevin were me, that's how he would have planned it. And so far he'd still be scoring a hundred percent. It seemed to boil down to a more sophisticated version of sending Jerry Hansen to me for advice, that other time.

The flaw in all this reasoning was that Kevin wasn't me. Kevin didn't operate on this sort of logic. He ran on instinct and sense of smell. I honestly believed that a plot of such complexity was beyond the capacity of his conscious mind. And yet it was sure enough happening the way I had it diagrammed on my chart. I was dealing with something else in Kevin: not a reasoned plan, but dark and secret currents somewhere down beneath the foam.

And if I wanted to survive one of Kevin's subliminal schemes, I was going to have to think and feel and be like Kevin. That was the thought I took to bed with me.

I slept very lightly and woke up at dawn. The sun was rising by the time I checked out of the hotel. I continued north on the coast road; it was not far to the border now. Again, my own little car was almost the only thing on the road.

But just past Ventimiglia, I did see some activity. A truck was parked on the shoulder, and a group of what I took at a glance to be *carabinieri* was prowling the slope above the highway. The men, five or six of them, were uniformed and carried automatic weapons. I went by too fast to be quite sure if they were military or civil. They didn't do my nerves any good either way.

However, there seemed to be no real cause for concern. A little short of Grimaldi I fell into a line of several sporty little cars, probably bound for Monaco from the looks of them. We reached the border between eight and nine, and the post was asleep, as I'd hoped it would be. None of the cars was pulled over, not even for a passport check.

Pas de problème.

The *autostrada* had now become the *autoroute*. I got back on it on the French side; it was time to pick up some speed. The Maritime Alps blocked this part of the route, and the French engineers had just blasted right through them. It made for fairly unnerving driving, especially since the road was fast. Wham, a tunnel; wham, daylight; wham, a tunnel again. To make it worse, I was having an ex post facto case of the jitters, even though I had no more frontiers to cross for the next few days.

The last set of machine-gunning *carabinieri* had got under my skin somehow. It had to be a trick of the fast-changing light, but every time I went into a tunnel I thought I saw muzzle flashes. Though I grew up around guns, I've never much liked them. The house on the farm was still full of them, and in the first bad weeks after Lauren had left, I'd wake up regularly around four in the morning, dry-mouthed and aching from a bourbon overdose, and find myself thinking about one gun or another. It was peculiar. The moment I woke, the picture of the gun would already be focused in my mind. There was no reason for it. I would not think about doing anything in particular with the gun. But I would have a desire to find it and touch it. The fact that I could handle it, load it, point it somewhere, pull the trigger, intrigued me endlessly as I lay on my back in the dark, waiting for the night to be over. It was all a little unsettling. When I finally quit drinking, it stopped.

If it started again now, I wasn't going to like it. In an effort to distract myself, I wound up thinking about the knife I'd given Kevin. Bad luck. I was convinced it was really bad luck now. But was it coming to him or me?

Then I was through the mountains at last. I took the highway north of Nice toward Lyon, Dijon, Calais. Someone in a serious hurry might have made the channel in a day, but I let it take me two. Time was not a critical factor, so far as I was concerned, though some might have said it should have been. My attitude wasn't completely tuned to the circumstances and I wasn't sure I wanted it to be. Somewhere a little better than halfway I made a buttonhook off the *autoroute* and found a tolerable hotel to spend the night in. I got a deluxe meal, which I could afford on the cheap franc, and forced a little conversation on the man who ran the place. My French, while not good, was a lot better than my Italian, and I wanted to brush it up some in case I needed it seriously in Belgium. In the morning I got up early and took off driving again.

I had not been in Calais before and I was looking forward to a pretty old seaport town. It had slipped my mind that the entire city had been bombed to dust during World War II. Rebuilt Calais was a quick job of jerry-rigging and ugly as sin. I checked into a no-star hotel, a hideous pile of brown concrete, and then went out to turn in the car. Walking back to the hotel, I stopped in a second-hand clothes store and bought a shirt, a tie, and a slightly seedy gray business suit. Back in my room, I put it all on before I went down to the dining room, where I had my worst meal yet in France. But I could watch myself in the mirrors that lined one wall, and I thought I looked about right — like a second-rate middle-aged businessman, too dull for anyone to bother about.

I caught a morning boat for Dover. It was a pleasant crossing, though the weather was a little iffy. There was a menacing shelf of purple cloud on the west horizon, and the water kept changing from green to gray. I thought we were probably making it just ahead of a storm. Most of the trip I spent sitting on the stern deck, where I drank a couple of stiff gins, the best the boat had to offer, to brace myself for customs. I had no story to explain why I couldn't open that briefcase. The gins helped, though, and by the time the chalk cliffs came into view I felt capable of ad-libbing if there was trouble. *Do what Kevin would do. Wing it.* There was no problem. I stated my intentions, tourism, and went through without a luggage check. Maybe the suit worked, or maybe they just weren't in the mood.

. . .

No more car rentals. I decided I wasn't up to driving on the wrong side of the road. I got a taxi and then caught the train for London. Aboard the train, I discovered how tired I finally was, and for maybe a couple of hours I slept. I woke up disoriented. It was peculiar to hear people around me speaking English again. That I could understand it didn't really seem to help.

I took the tube from Victoria to Paddington, remembering that there was a lot of cheap lodging around the second station. In the lobby I picked up a handful of rooming house flyers and took them to a pub counter to go through. Most of them were twelve-pound-a-night bed-and-breakfasts, riddled with curfews and visitor restrictions. They would not do. Then there was an ad for "efficiency flats," by day or by week, a nice glossy brochure, with fish-eye photographs in color. "Suitable for military personnel," it said.

The place was just off Leinster Square, an easy walk from the station. The entrance was not nearly so prepossessing as the flyer might have led me to expect, but I was tired and in a hurry and hadn't believed the flyer in the first place. I went in and negotiated. The best lies are the ones that have the most truth built into them, and I told the manager (a lady of a certain age) that I was a film editor and (with a judicious amount of winking and smirking) that though I was traveling on a tourist visa I was actually scouting for work. I would be in and out, possibly absent for a week or more at a stretch, but I wanted the place nailed down for a month. Cash in advance, provided she was willing to make a minor adjustment in the weekly rate, which, after some argument, she was.

I paid up, claimed my key, and went up the stairs. To call the place a flat of any kind was a masterpiece of euphemism. There was one room and a tiny bath. The kitchen facilities consisted of a hot plate and a miniature refrigerator, which did, I was pleased to note, contain a couple of ice trays. There were two dingy armchairs, a small table edged with cigarette burns, where a plain dial telephone sat, and a window which was painted shut. The bed folded into the wall, and a smell of mildew leaked from its niche. The place would have made a good set for a suicide.

I went out. There were plenty of other little hotels in Leinster Square and Prince's Square, but none of them would have been any better. On the Bayswater Road, near the corner of Kensington Gardens, I foud a booze shop and bought a quart of dark naval rum. Circling back around Queensway, I picked up some plastic cups at a grocer's and then I went back to the room.

It was time to get drunk and think it over. The old ice in the trays was flecked and gray, but the rum camouflaged that nicely. I had a couple of belts and pounded on the window until I could open it. It was warm out, even for July, and clear. With some difficulty, I let down the bed. To accomplish that, the chairs had to be moved against the far wall. I dragged the table around to the head of the bed and set up the bottle and an ashtray within easy reach, then took off my shoes and lay down.

Halfway down my second cup of rum I began to feel a lot better. The jolly tar smiled at me from the bottle; he looked like a friendly sort. With the lights off I could forget the room and see only the darkening square of the window, and past it a single waving branch and a patch of sky. I was reasonably pleased with myself, so far. No one of any importance had the foggiest notion where I was anymore, and that made me happy, though for no clear reason. Since I hadn't been visaed in France, it would take even Interpol an extra few minutes to pin me down. An enterprising person with the right connections could always trace me through the car rental, but I didn't think that would apply to Kevin either way. So far as Kevin was concerned, I might as well have dropped off the face of the earth.

Would Kevin be worrying about me at all, though? I really

doubted that. If he already knew I'd picked up the relay from Lauren, he probably wouldn't be anything but pleased. He'd assume, in that half-conscious way of his, that things had worked out just the way he'd planned. He wouldn't be fretting over me at all. It was maddening. When I hit the halfway mark on the rum bottle, it began to be sad too.

Why me? Why not Kevin? Why not both of us together? It wasn't only a matter of wishing he'd do his own dirty work and leave me out. I actually missed the son of a bitch, strange as that might sound. Eyes closed, I constructed a montage of all the things we'd done together: shoots that ran for sleepless weeks, panic edits, late-night scheming of one thing or another, be it a movie or the real thing. Kevin's quick flashes of insight that cut through so many difficulties. If he was a plague to me, he'd always been an inspiration too, and in a mood like this one, when I rode on the familiar adrenal surge that preceded the first serious move of any of our games, I wanted him with me or at least on my side. During the long charged moment when whatever we'd been brewing was finally committed to action, it had always seemed that nothing could come between us. I did miss him. I knew I could do the job without him, believed I could do it against him if it had to be that way, but it wasn't going to be half as much fun.

13

THE MAIL CALL at American Express was the scariest thing on my agenda yet, enough so that my legs got rubbery during the walk from the tube to the office, and a couple of times they even tried to swivel out from under me and turn back. This time there really was something tangible to worry about. My only safety net was that those address labels were typed Italian style, with some minor variations on the spelling of my name, but that was thin. Extremely thin. It might just barely be enough to get me out of an indictment, but only after long hours or maybe days and weeks of slow frying in various interrogation rooms. I wasn't looking forward to any of that.

But I went ahead to the office and once I was there it occurred to me that the box might not even have arrived yet, what with the Italian mail and all. But it had. The girl handling the mail that day looked to be about sixteen and was as cute as a button, reedy thin with honey-colored hair hanging down to her waist, and she didn't appear to be the suspicious type. She forked over the package with a smile and no questions. I dropped it into a shopping bag I'd brought along in hopes that everything would work out this way, and then I got the hell out of there.

Clean as a whistle. For luck, I went straight over to Paddington Station. It seemed just as well if I put some space between picking up the box and booking my next passage to faraway romantic places. I dropped the parcel in the Paddington checkroom and then walked back down to Leinster Square. Up in the rented flat again, I sat down and wrote that letter I'd promised Mimmo. Then I remembered I probably couldn't afford to mail it.

That pretty well took care of the serious business for the day. I went out and had a big soggy pub lunch and then went to the Islamic Room of the British Museum, where I killed most of the afternoon looking at incomprehensible calligraphy and things like that. Toward evening, I went back to American Express and booked on the next morning's boat-train to Brussels. I'd thought of asking Miss Blondie out for a drink, but she seemed to have clocked out for the day, and besides, the Brits don't talk to strangers much, and besides that, it would have been a poor moment, strategically speaking, to break my solitude.

So the next morning it was back to Dover, the reverse of the very same train ride I'd made two days before. If I wasn't in the jet set, I was at least in the wheel set, or something like that. This time around I was prepared with an armload of newspapers and magazines. English, English, English. I gobbled it down. It didn't matter very much that the news was not terrifically interesting for its own sweet sake. I hadn't had any English for weeks and I didn't know how long it might be before I got a chance to have any more.

This time around I was booked on a hydrofoil instead of the boat. It was faster but at the same time more boring. There was no deck. We were all strapped into our seats as if on an airplane. The water and sky spun by outside like a one-shot ribbon of film. I wanted to sleep but I was too jumpy for that. When the duty-free offer was made, I bought a good bottle of vodka for Racine.

It was at Ostend that the worst finally did happen, or almost. I got myself pulled out of the line over money, or at least that was the initial problem. So far as Belgian customs was concerned, it seemed that I had too much of it for the plausibility of my stated duration of visit (two weeks to a month) and purpose of visit (tourism, yet again). Two inspectors beckoned me not to a private room but simply to one side of the line for a more extensive conversation. They were speaking to each other in Flemish, which tended to rattle me. I might have followed their general drift in any of the Romance languages, but Flemish left me with no clue at all.

Of course there was a perfectly reasonable explanation of the money situation, which even had the virtue of relative truth: I was taking a long trip through several countries, I had earned money in Italy and converted it to traveler's checks for ease and safety of transport, et cetera, et cetera. But my delivery was off and in the middle of it I noticed that, sure enough, my hands had begun to shake, and one of the customs men had already noticed it too. I'd had it. The second customs officer was already rooting through my shoulder bag while the first one, who spoke clumsy but authoritative English, recommended that I open the Halliburton.

It was as if someone had slapped me or dumped a bucket of ice water over my head. I calmed down at once.

"So sorry," I said. "I'm afraid that will take up a lot of your time."

"How?" said the customs man. He was rather unpleasant looking, I thought: yellow and lean, with a brush cut and an obnoxious pencil-line mustache.

"You see, the locks are broken," I said. On a sudden inspiration, I set the combination dials to six digits of my New York phone number and snapped at the catches. Nothing happened, to be sure.

"So," the customs man said. He was the laconic type, in English anyway. He tried the catches himself. Nothing doing.

"It's been that way since yesterday," I said. "Rust, maybe. I've had no time to repair it. If you could find a locksmith . . ."

"Hm," the customs man said. His partner had reclosed my shoulder bag. "And the contents?"

"Oh, only papers," I said, with what I hoped was a hearty smile. After all, the statement was true in the literal sense. "Business papers, of no great interest to anyone but me."

There was a brief exchange in Flemish. I decided it was time to push my luck a hair.

"Of course I realize you can't very well just take my word for this," I said. "And I will have to have it repaired very soon in any case. Only I would prefer not to damage the bag itself, it was rather expensive, you see. But if there is a locksmith nearby . . . Of course I understand you have to inspect the contents. Only I do hope that I won't miss my train . . ."

The customs men spoke again in Flemish as I continued to babble in this vein. Finally the English speaker silenced me with a raised hand.

"Not necessary," he said. He handed me back my bags and waved me through.

Kevin would have been proud of me for that one, I thought, and I did my best to be proud of myself, but that life-saving surge of confidence was gone now, as if it had never been. I was so limp that I literally stumbled as I moved out toward the train platforms, and finally I stopped and propped myself up on what turned out to be a letter drop. Once I noticed that, it occurred to me that it would be safe enough to mail Mimmo's letter here; the Ostend postmark would be sufficiently misleading. So I slipped it in. *Bonne chance*, Mimmo. Then I looked over the signs and plotted my course out to the Brussels train.

It was the late afternoon of a splendidly clear day and here in the north the air still tasted of spring. My spoke of the platform was empty; it appeared that I was the only one off that particular boat who was bound for the city of Brussels. Amber sunlight came tilting from the west, wrapping over the old green train, which was already sitting in the station, though the doors were locked. I smoked cigarette after cigarette while I waited (nothing like a brush with death or danger to make them really taste good) and the fabric of smoke coiled around me like an animate cage, the only life in the motionless air, the sun shocking it through with color.

Ten or fifteen minutes passed, and I saw a trio of people approaching from the station end of the platform, slowly as figures in a mirage of some kind. They came nearer, and I saw they were a family or looked like one: father, mother and a teenage daughter, all burdened down with too many suitcases. The man began to ask me in awkward French whether this was the train to Brussels, and when I replied in English I was rewarded by all their obvious relief. They were American, Southerners like me, it developed, and we talked a little while we waited for the train to open. The daughter said nothing, but she was very pretty, with hair so brilliantly red that unconsciously I almost reached out to touch and fondle it, before I realized what consternation that surely would have caused. I wondered at the impulse, naturally, but it was not until later, when the train had finally been unlocked and I withdrew to my own musty green compartment, that I understood it was Lauren whom that quiet girl's hair had so reminded me of.

It was not so far from the Gare du Midi to the Rue d'Irlande, where Racine lived now. I made a couple of wrong turns, walking up the hill in the dark, but I did find the place without using a map. It was an old abandoned bar Racine had rebuilt to live in, and there was still some of the bar's lettering on the big plate-glass window in front, though not enough to decipher. Tonight the window was dark and there was no answer to my ring.

I had not let Racine know that I was coming, but somehow

I was certain that he would be in town all the same. He conducted a great deal of his business in bars and cafés and I'd probably arrived at a poor part of the evening to catch him in. Since for once I seemed to be in a daring mood, I decided to go ahead and seek ingress. The place was on the corner. I went around the side street to the right. There was a one-story wall there which looked to be climbable. I slung the bags over it and scrambled up after them. On the other side was a low roof with a heavy fiber-glass skylight set in it. The sheets of glass had been fixed in the frame with silicon caulk and it was easy enough to loosen one. I lowered my bags and then dropped down into the house.

Now I was in a little catty-cornered tiled room, roofed over entirely with fiber glass. There was a drain in the middle of the floor. Back when the place had operated as a bar, this area had been an open courtyard on the way to the *pissoir*, which was off to my left. A door to the right let into the main part of the house. I went in and stopped for a moment to listen. It was dark and quiet and there was no sign of movement. I padded into the little kitchen and groped for the light switch. Nobody there. Someone's dinner dishes had been left in the sink. I pulled the duty-free vodka out of my bag and stuck it in the freezer.

A stairway back to the kitchen led up to the bedroom, the only room on the second floor. I tiptoed up, lest Racine or someone be asleep, but there was no one. Nothing to do but wait a while. I opened a Stella Artois I found in the refrigerator, and repositioned the glass in the low ceiling. Then I lit a cigarette and strolled out into the big front room, which was full of sound equipment, but mainly with all of Racine's horns.

Racine was not the same Racine of the French classical theater, of course, nor was he any relation, so far as I knew. The name was very likely an assumed one, though he'd been using it for some time and I'd never known him by any other. It was probably not the same name under which, according to one rumor, he was listed as a terrorist on the Interpol computer. It might or might not have been the name he was using when, according to another rumor, he'd spent a few days sighting a silenced rifle on the ear of some Common Market dignitary, never quite making up his mind to pull the trigger.

I wasn't sure I really believed that last story anyway, though it was the sort of tale that tended to crop up around Racine. The terrorist bit derived from a couple of minor raps from ten or fifteen years before — a knife one time, a hot car another — the sort of thing that would make you a probable in the eyes of almost any Western European police force. None of it really fit well with the Racine I knew from New York, a quiet equable man so patient and even-tempered that I had almost never seen anything unsettle him.

People do sometimes change, of course. *Mais plus ça change* . . .

It happened that Kevin had been the one to dig him up originally. Kevin had heard an obscure foreign release of one of Racine's tapes on WQXR and decided that it had the perfect *je ne sais quoi* for the soundtrack to something we were working on at the time. With the persistence he could sometimes summon when he got truly hung up on something, he wrote to the station and then to a Paris music publisher and to several other places too, finally to discover that Racine had been living on the Lower East Side, more or less our neighbor, the whole time.

So Kevin did finally get the tape he wanted, but he and Racine never really hit it off. They were *too* much opposites of each other, I suppose. Racine was deliberate, phlegmatic almost, and also in those days his English was not good. Kevin, with his fast-changing moods and general impatience, must have looked like some sort of leaping insect to him. For me it was different. There was something in Racine's even pace that appealed to me from the very beginning, so I kept on calling him after Kevin had quit. Over the three or four years he spent in New York Racine's name as a sax player began to be known in a small but significant way, chiefly among back-room cognoscenti, while I remained a less erudite fan. By the time he cleared out for Brussels we knew and trusted each other well enough that, for example, I didn't think he'd be upset that I'd broken into his apartment full of horns.

There were a lot now, more than I remembered, ranged in a row of stands along the wall. He'd always had the tenor, the alto, the soprano, but now there were several more on either side of those three, whose exact names I couldn't have really called. Great old big ones and little old bitty ones . . . Racine must be prospering in Belgium, I thought, picking up the smallest horn, a miniaturized sax just slightly bigger than the palm of my hand. There was a click behind me, from the rear of the apartment, and I felt a cold pulse in the small of my back that told me I was certainly being watched. Maybe some-one had been asleep somewhere after all.

"*T'inquiète pas*," I called out. "It's only me." I turned around. Nothing, though the door in the glassed-over atrium was ajar, when I thought for sure I'd shut it. Of course it might have drifted open on its own. The sound might have been a mouse or something too, though I really didn't think so. I set the little horn back on its stand, so as to have both hands free. The door swung all the way open and Racine came into the room.

It seemed like a sort of lengthy moment, and I wondered if maybe I should have behaved like a normal person and called before I'd come. Racine did not seem to have changed a bit, I had time to observe. He was a short man, well under my own height, but wiry and always in the very best of shape. In his younger days he'd been an acrobat, and he still looked it. He had blunt features of the kind people like to call Gallic, and kept his hair cut to stubble against his skull. Tonight he was wearing a plain gray shirt and trousers that looked a little like a uniform, with a multicolored scarf wound several times around his neck.

"*Bienvenu*," Racine said finally. He walked across the room and kissed me on the cheek. Custom of the country. I returned the gesture.

"Sorry about that," I said. "Maybe I should have knocked. Actually I did but there wasn't anybody home."

"No, it's okay," Racine said, and now he really did seem completely unconcerned. "You like a beer maybe?"

We moved into the kitchen, where I put my bottle on top of the refrigerator with the other empties and took another beer. Racine sat down at the square wooden table in the middle of the room.

"You want some vodka?" I said. "It's probably not quite cold yet."

"Me wait," Racine said. His English was good now, a hell of a lot better than my French, for one thing, but he sometimes didn't bother declining pronouns. I joined him at the table.

"I came in through the roof, which I guess you figured out," I said. "Probably I should have put a note on the door or something."

"No problem. Only I see the lights on coming down the street. So I decide to come in the back way myself, you know?"

"Sure," I said. "I'll get some silicon and close it up for you."

"Not serious."

"It'll leak, though."

"True." Racine leaned back in his chair. He spoke English very softly, rounding off the corners of the words. "So. How are you doing?"

"Passing through," I said. "Thought I'd stop in and say hello."

"Good. You like to stay?"

"A few days, maybe. If you can handle that. I have money, though, enough for a hotel."

"No. Stay here. There's no one else around. I have a mattress for the room in front."

"Well, thanks then."

"No, it's been a long time since you were here. Two years about, no?"

"Almost," I said. "You're looking good, anyway. Got some new brass out there I see."

Racine smiled. "Not so badly. I'm a little bit a local hero now."

"Congratulations," I said. "When's the U.S. tour?"

"Soon, I hope." Shrugging, Racine got up and went to the refrigerator. He drank a lot of beer and drank it fast too, though it never seemed to do him that much damage. He offered me another but I waved it away. Brussels beer can be a bit tricky, though Stella, as I recalled, was fairly safe.

"There's been talk about that," Racine said. "Nothing definite. And you?"

"Same old jive," I said. "I just cut a documentary in Rome, so I thought I'd roll around some before I went back home."

"Nice. What about?"

"Junkies," I said. "Ex-junkies, I should say. It wasn't much good of a picture."

Racine lit a Gauloise and flicked the square blue pack across the table in my direction.

"Lauren?" he said. I took a cigarette.

"Comme ci, comme ça," I said. Now it was my turn to shrug.

"You're here on business, or just for fun?"

"I don't know," I said. "What if it turned out to be business?"

"Not a film."

"No." Racine knew a little bit about the underside of our endeavors, though not really all that much, I didn't think. "Remember, I can stay in a hotel if it should happen to be more convenient that way. I was just in the neighborhood, like I said."

"No, we're friends," Racine said. "Stay here. Just —"

"*Compris,*" I said, and it was too. I would do my damnedest not to expose him to any risk, including no contraband on the premises, and like that. The arrangement was simple, it didn't even have to be directly discussed, and it made me quite happy. I found it pleasant, for a change, to be around someone it was so uncomplicated to trust.

13

LIKED BRUSSELS. Though I'd only been there once before I had fond memories of the place. It seemed to me to be an undemanding city, far less intimidating to the relative stranger than Paris or Rome or even London. It was uncomplicated to get around, partly because if I went anywhere very far Racine went with me as a rule. If I did end up on my own, at least people were a lot more tolerant of my pidgin French than they would have been anywhere — in France, for instance.

So it was easy, indeed very pleasant, to spend a couple of days just hanging out. Racine was not too busy, it seemed, so we spent a good deal of time doing not much. He took me to the Wiertz Museum to look at peculiar paintings and to the Natural History Museum to inspect the bones of dinosaurs. We ate big lunches, then slept them off on the grass of the parks. Like good lotus eaters, we devoted some serious attention to actual food, and Brussels is a good place for that, from local specialties like *tomates aux crevettes* to the couscous made by the Moroccans and Algerians who lived in Racine's quarter.

A good city for food, it was an even better one for beer. Racine's beer tour was famous; at any rate it had almost killed me on my previous visit there. This time around I was better prepared for the sneaky qualities of the Belgian mixes, so I was never taken entirely by surprise. All the same we had a few long nights. Brussels has a couple of cafés on every block and Racine seemed to know a few people in all of them. I trailed along behind him, falling back on nods and smiles whenever my French gave out, getting myself shamefully beaten at billiards or, more often, bumper pool, the premier café game of the town. On the shank of the night we'd usually end up at some club where Racine's musical friends were playing, and sometimes, if I was lucky, he'd sit in.

It was the first really carefree time I'd had in months, so it was easy enough to forget what I'd really come to Brussels for. I'd hit the middle of Kevin's bracket, and there was time to fool around with. And soon the thought of the little chore ahead of me was not really a memory at all anymore; it came to me more as a sort of dull pressure, like the opening phase of a headache. Maybe it was the beer that did that, or maybe it was a period of extraordinary success with my Kevin imitation. But I'd stopped thinking consciously about the deal at all.

Then one morning Racine got up quite a lot earlier than had become our habit. I heard him banging around in the kitchen around eight in the morning, the noise of pots and pans slowly penetrating my dream of sailing a sea of the cherry-flavored beer we'd been drinking the night before. But I was still plugged into my mattress by the time Racine was ready to go. He told me he had a rehearsal, dropped a spare key on the mattress between my feet, and went out.

As luck would have it I tripped over the Halliburton on the way to the bathroom. It popped my little toe out of joint, the one I'd snagged in a sparring accident one afternoon some years before, and I had to sit down and painfully snap it back into place. Not the best of starts for my day. I made a cup of espresso and carried it out to the front room, where I stood looking out the big bar window. It was a market day and the women of the quarter were carrying their string bags and baskets down the street toward the square.

I got dressed and checked my pocket date book. Last day of the bracket. I think I'd known that all along, somewhere down the winding spirals of my unconscious mind.

So. I worked out, took a shower, got dressed again. Back at the front window, I could see that the sky had clouded over suddenly. Maybe it was going to rain, a common event in Brussels.

I went into the kitchen and cleaned the coffee pot. The clock on the kitchen wall said nine forty-five.

It might turn out to be a long day, I thought.

Then it was sunny again on the street. I decided to go for a walk. Since the weather seemed so iffy, I took an umbrella along. But it was not yet raining, though it was cold for summer. At the Porte de Halle I stopped for a moment and stared at the round medieval tower there, a windowless, weathered silo. To the south, a block down the Chaussée de Waterloo, a new subway stop was noisily under construction. Racine had told me that all the noise came from a gigantic refrigeration unit; it seemed that the sandy soil of Brussels had to be frozen before it was solid enough to dig in. A curious enterprise. Though the line was complete in one direction, a subway ride did not entice me. I walked north toward the Grand' Place.

What I really wanted to look at was Manneken-Pis, just a shade south of the Grand' Place at a minor intersection in an obscure niche. For a long time, ever since the first time I had seen it, it had been my favorite city monument anywhere, partly because of its lack of ostentation. The little bronze reminded one not of a cherub or cupid but of an authentic human infant, peeing into the small fountain below the niche; I probably was imagining the trace of a smile and wink I saw around his greening features. Not nearly so grand as the Trevi Fountain, but maybe a little truer. It was here above all other places that I was impressed with the great age of Europe and the fact that its people do conduct a daily life amid the visible and palpable evidence of the centuries. It deserved to take centuries for any capital to learn to construct its symbol so exactly on the human scale.

The old joke goes that mankind was invented by water for its transportation from one place to another. Another curious enterprise. Well, wasn't it the truth?

Then the weather finally did break and it was rainwater splashing in the fountain now. I opened my umbrella and walked up to the Grand' Place after all. The rain had cleared the square and I was almost alone, turning round and round on the rain-slicked cobbles, peering out from the black rim of my umbrella and trying to remember which one of those lunging Gothic buildings was the Amigo. It had been called that since the days of Spanish rule, when it was the city prison, when the soldiers addressed you as "amigo" when they took you by the shoulder to lead you there.

The jail had been moved by this time, naturally. I could quit while I was ahead, or else I stood a good chance of finding out where they had moved it to.

Back at Racine's place, I dug out the number Lauren had given me and dialed. There wasn't any answer, though. Not for the rest of the day. It dawned on me then that if the other end of this transaction was a traveling man like myself I just might have missed the connection altogether. And that thought was a comfort, in its way.

Racine was up and out early again the next morning, on the same mission as before, so I had the house all to myself, and the telephone too. I had stopped believing anything was ever going to come of that number, but I'd already dialed it enough to have it memorized, so I gave it another spin. What do you know, somebody picked it up before it even rang at my end. I was so startled I didn't even say hello.

"*Qui est-ce?*" the voice said. A man. There was a little pause and then he said something in a language I didn't recognize. Something Slavic, possibly. On a hunch I said nothing and waited to hear what would happen.

"Who is, pliss?" the voice said, in densely accented English. "Who is?"

I hung up. Something about that voice had been familiar, but it was irritatingly just beyond my range of recognition. I thought about it for a half hour, drinking a Stella in hopes it might loosen up my memory. It didn't. I called again. Another quick pickup and the French salutation; it was almost like they were expecting something.

"*Anne Morrison regrette qu'elle ne peut pas venir,*" I said. "*Mais je suis son ami . . . et je suis venu pour finir son affaire, ça va?*"

"*Vraiment?*" the voice said. I heard muttering in the background.

"Spik American, pliss?" the voice said.

I started laughing. Couldn't help it.

"Why you laugh for?" the voice said. Very suspicious. I wiped that smile off my face.

"Nothing," I said. "Only, in America we call it English."

"Is not same language, no?"

"No," I said. "I guess not. Well? Do we meet?"

"No. Give your number, we call you."

"But I am in a café," I said.

"Then which might be your hotel?"

"I only just arrived," I said, improvising. "I have no hotel so far."

Another pause.

"Call back one hour," the voice finally said. I agreed to that and hung up.

* * *

Deadlock over my phone number went on for the rest of the day. I talked to the accented voice several times, and it remained very stubborn. It wanted the number, I presumed, so it could trace it and check me out. But I wasn't giving Racine's number away, and I couldn't think of any workable way to use a different one. My proposal was a neutral meeting place, but the voice kept saying no to that. By the fourth call I was getting impatient.

"Anne will be sad if you don't get the present she sent," I said. "Do you want me to have to send it back to her?"

"No, of course," the voice said. "Also there is a present here for her."

"It brings good luck to exchange gifts," I said, a little facetiously. There was more whispering beside the other phone.

"Call back one hour, pliss."

"The hell with you guys," I said as I hung up. But when I did call back the voice made a date with me at an address on the Rue des Capucins for noon the following day.

It all started out in the wrong way, because it seemed that Racine didn't have a rehearsal scheduled for that morning. I'd slept in more or less on purpose, but when I woke up he was still in the house, and he wasn't dressed to go out. At first I thought little of that. I went into the tiled atrium and stretched and worked out, about double the usual. Something about my plans for the day made that seem like a good thing to do. Racine was practicing in the front room; I could hear the muffled horn from time to time over the sound of my accelerated breathing.

I took a shower and wandered back into the apartment. Racine suggested a café breakfast, but I pleaded letters to write. Racine put on a headset, sat down in front of his wall of tape decks, and began to noodle around on a sopranino sax, occasionally reaching forward to adjust a dial. I took a position at the kitchen table and tried to think of someone among my acquaintances so innocent and so harmless that I wouldn't mind letting him know I was in Brussels. After about an hour of that I took blank sheets of paper, folded them into two envelopes, and addressed them left-handed in block capitals to Kevin and Lauren.

"Post office," I said to Racine, heading for the door. He pushed the headphones back and lowered the horn.

"I could lend you some stamps," he said.

"I need to stock up. It's not much of a walk." And I slipped out. Passing along the outside of the window, I saw that Racine had not resumed playing the horn, though he'd put the headphones on again. He'd shifted his chair to face the window, but somehow our eyes didn't seem to meet.

Rue des Capucins was part of the derelict snarl of streets down the hill to the west of the Palais de Justice. The slope was a steep one and the streets were shady and dark, even a little cold, it seemed. At the east end of every street the view up the hill was completely blocked by the wall of the Palais, which seemęd to suck all the light from the sky. I recalled an apocryphal report that the building's architect had either jumped or hung himself from the dome on the day of its completion.

The address they'd given me turned out to be a café with no name, only a number. Even the term *café* was a little grand for these circumstances, but that is what they called them. I knew the quarter and I wasn't surprised, had even dressed my shabbiest for the occasion. The goddamn Halliburton stuck out like a flare, however. Most of the clientele had left the whole concept of suitcases behind years before. I ordered a Stella and the siege began. Belgian winos are not nearly so shy and retiring as the kind we have in the States, or at least not if you're in one of their bars. They get right in your face and stay there till you've surrendered whatever it is they want, be it a drink or a smoke or some change. Or else you have to hit them, or something. Without the bag I might have passed, but I couldn't very well have come without it.

So I bought a drink for a grizzled old soak with what looked to be a recently broken nose, and set him up in a chair next to mine. I couldn't understand his patois, but he made a nice buffer between me and most of the others. Five minutes passed, then fifteen. There was nobody around who could have been who I was looking for. Everyone in the place was too old and too thoroughly marinated for the part.

When the guy finally did show he appeared from the back, so I didn't spot him until he came up to the bar. He was younger than anyone else, including me, probably around nineteen or twenty. An unnecessarily tall guy, with longish shaggy hair hanging around an urgent lupine face, a big wedge of bone set in a stubbly neck. At first glance I thought he might be the one, and I got a chance to look him over in more detail, because he ordered a beer and sat down to my left. I didn't much care for the looks of him, really. He was so tall and emaciated he seemed to have been stretched, and the effect was a little ghoulish. To cap it off, on his right hand he wore a massive silver ring in the shape of a skull with a vulture perched on top of it, wings outspread toward the palm side of his finger. Another silver skull, sans vulture, swung on a two-inch chain from his right ear. Not exactly the Brussels look, I didn't think. He wasn't the most prepossessing thing I'd seen all day, even taking the locale into account, but I was pretty sure he was my man, and I was right.

"Vous êtes l'ami de —" he said.

"Anne Morrison," I finished the sentence.

He drank off his beer in three long gulps, stubbly Adam's apple bobbling. I saw him scope out the Halliburton, which was sitting on the floor with my foot on it.

"Yonko," he said. I took that to be his name.

"Alfred," I said. Why bother with the truth? Yonko pushed his glass away and stood, beckoning me with a gesture of his thumb. I picked up the briefcase and followed him toward a door in the rear of the place. The room we entered was generously proportioned for a closet, but a bit on the small side for anything else. There was hardly room for the three bar chairs that had been put in it. The third party, a short man with blondish frizzy hair and a bald spot, was already seated in one of them, with a sort of Alpine rucksack between his knees. Since there was little room to stand I sat across from him; Yonko took the remaining chair.

"Grushko," Yonko said, indicating his companion, who looked up and smiled. I knew him. I knew I knew him but not how or where from . . . it was connected with the familiarity of that accent, somehow. I gaped at him like a fish, and then I had it. *He was Dario's cameraman, how do you like that.* Tumblers began to turn over in my head; this was a new combination.

"Alfred," I said. Grushko nodded and smiled. If he knew or recalled what my real name was he gave no sign of it. Now I vividly remembered that rather feckless air he had about him that had irritated me so much the single time we'd met before. What had Mimmo told me? I only remembered that Grushko didn't speak English and came, in the first place, from Bulgaria. Where skull-shaped accessories were no doubt the very latest thing among the young.

Grushko, smiling happily, said something to Yonko in what I now assumed was Bulgarian, and Yonko left the room. Grushko and I sat in forcedly amiable silence for the five or so minutes he was gone. It was close in the little room and I was beginning to sweat. I supposed Yonko was checking to see if I had any cohorts waiting in the wings. When he returned he said something which must have been the all-clear, because Grushko went on nodding and smiling.

"Now," Yonko said to me, switching over to his version of "American." "We show? You try?"

I nodded. Yonko stretched out a hand for the Halliburton

and I let him have it. Grushko opened the top of the rucksack and pushed it across the floor to me. Inside were a lot of heavy plastic bags full of a crystalline white powder. Yes, it did look like cocaine. I opened the third one. Grushko, meanwhile, had passed a slip of paper to Yonko, who began to tinker with the combination dials on the briefcase. The taste of the dust was not too familiar to me, but then it had been a while. I scooped up a reasonable finger full, gave it a hearty snort, and sat back.

Not much effect at first, only a slight numbness. Yonko was having some difficulty with the briefcase locks, it seemed. I was beginning to think I had a knapsack full of benzocaine on my hands. Then it hit, a blue flame roaring out of my vitals into my limbs and head, rocking me back in the chair for a moment. Silence — I heard the locks of the Halliburton snapping back at last and knew that Yonko was now getting an eyeful of the display I'd fixed up for him in Rome — but I no longer cared about any of that because I was already throwing myself clumsily across the room at Grushko, clutching at his lapels and the skin of his neck, hissing at him, though I knew he couldn't understand, "Why you bastards, you bastards, it's heroin."

I had taken just enough heroin in the past to know I should never, ever, take any more, but I was sure enough of the effects, one of which is to make you feel a great deal smarter, stronger, and quicker than you really are. That might help explain some of what happened next. Grushko and I fell over in our chairs and, rolling out, I saw Yonko reaching for a folded raincoat in the corner. He'd moved so quickly that the open briefcase was tumbling out of the chair, spilling the sugar frosting of real cash and scattering the bundles of chopped-up Italian magazines, which I'd arranged so carefully underneath, in a wide fan and flutter all over the floor. They weren't supposed to be seeing that yet, it was planned as a variation on the old

bait-and-switch, but it wasn't going to be anything now —
Yonko was going for a weapon, I assumed, so I threw a single
arm block at his hand, missed, and tore up my trick elbow.
It was bad enough that I could feel it even through the scag,
and that frightened me, so I sat back on the floor, clutching
where it hurt. When I looked up again Yonko had a small
submachine gun, I couldn't have told you what brand, pointed
right at my nose.

It was a tense moment, even though I was too whacked out
to be as much affected by it as I otherwise might have been.
Another effect of heroin is that nothing, nothing at all, matters
very much during the rush. I felt terrific, though intellectually
I understood that my position was poor. Grushko spoke to
Yonko sharply in Bulgarian, collected the baggies and put them
back in the rucksack, and slipped out of the room. Yonko
glanced at his watch and stood, motioning me to get up also.

"Look," I said. "This is a simple misunderstanding . . ."

Yonko didn't respond. He just wasn't my kind of person. I
began to feel slightly depressed in spite of the dope. I hate
machine guns, especially in the hands of irresponsible people.
Maybe it would really have been better if they had thought of
the right way to arrest me back there at the Rome airport when
I arrived.

"Take up the bag," Yonko said shortly, checking his watch
again. There seemed no point in complaining about the quality
of his "American." I lifted the rucksack and slung it over my
left shoulder, leaving my good arm free on the off chance I'd
get an opportunity to use it for anything. Yonko draped the
raincoat over his gun and waved me toward the door. I stepped
out into the main room of the café with him following close
behind. My arm had stopped hurting for the moment, and
the scag gave me a weird detachment from the whole predicament, though in a distant way I realized that it wasn't getting
any better. The people in the café didn't seem very interested
in us just then, though I thought we had to be showing a little

strain. I wondered if Yonko would really have the nerve to pull the trigger if I dove in among the crowded tables, say, but I didn't quite have the nerve myself to try.

Then we were out on the street and my heart sank some more when I saw Grushko in the driver's seat of a blue Peugeot, pulled up to the curb. If I went anywhere in that car I was quite sure I would never come back, and Yonko was already urging me into the back seat. I opened the rear door and turned around. Yonko was standing back, well out of my reach. He wasn't entirely stupid, I had to give him that. Up and down, the street was very empty. I looked up at the Palais de Justice, but no one was looking back down, of course. It was my last chance for a break, but Yonko could probably shoot me more conveniently here than he could have done in the bar.

Then there was a sort of spitting noise and Yonko clapped his left hand to his right shoulder, lowering the gun long enough for me to reach him. I hit his wrist with a low block — got it right this time — and booted the gun under the car. Yonko backed up against the wall of the café; he was bleeding from the right shoulder, and for the moment, off the count. Grushko was staring at him round-eyed from behind the wheel of the car, and I decided that I'd bet my money that he either didn't have a gun or couldn't hit a moving target. With the rucksack still over my shoulder, I ran down the block to where Racine, improbably, was waiting.

"A souvenir or what?" I said.

It was a good deal later, and I was admiring the little silenced sniper rifle, which broke down into three sections small enough to fit into an innocuous cardboard tube. In fact, the camouflage was so good that Racine had insisted on taking me by a doctor's to check the elbow (over my protest, to be sure) before we even went home to drop the stuff. But the medical news was favorable: no important new damage to the joint; a week of hot water and Ace bandages and I'd be all right.

"From the old days of *la politique*," Racine said.

"Get much use out of it back then?"

"I was only keeping it for a friend."

"Sure." I looked down the sight, a telescope with cross hairs.

"No, it's true," Racine said. "Once I did think of some use for it. But, I didn't."

"Well, you've got a flair for trick shooting, anyway," I said, handing him the sight.

"I think it needs adjustment. I intended to kill him."

Racine packed the pieces of gun into the tube.

"You don't know how much worse that makes me feel," I said. "What made you decide to follow me, by the way?"

"One doesn't always take a suitcase to the post office," Racine said. "Besides, it is the other way from the way you went."

"Well, don't think I don't appreciate it," I said. *"Bien obligé."*

"De rien," Racine said. He tucked the tube under his arm and walked out of the kitchen, where we'd been unwinding with the aid of a little beer and vodka, into the tiled atrium. I went after him. A good-sized tile was missing from a spot halfway up the wall and Racine was slipping the tube into the hole behind it.

"I think I might be beginning to understand something," I said. "That night I broke in —" Those little clicks I'd thought I'd heard were falling into the pattern now. A person armed with a pocketknife could slit the flexible caulking and get into that hidey-hole rather quickly . . .

"Only a precaution," Racine said. "You're not offended?"

"Bien sûr que non," I said.

"And now you understand also why I have silicon around."

"Yes," I said. "Quite so."

"There is room to unload the pack in here too, I think."

I hesitated.

"You know something?" I said.

"What?"

"This might not be such a good time to be my friend."

Racine lit a cigarette. "Why not?" he said. "It's when you need one."

"True for you," I said, and later when we'd caulked the gun and the dope up into the wall and started to talk over some details of the matter, it occurred to me that, sentimental considerations aside, he really did have a point.

14

HEN A RATHER SILLY thing happened, which was that I got sick. It wasn't immediately obvious what the problem was. After my little runaround with Grushko and Yonko, I'd expected to feel pretty bad for a few days. One of the especially unpleasant things about heroin is the hangover, which is fully as intense as the rush and lasts a lot longer — from three days to a week. I felt as though my entire body had been crushed under an enormous anvil, which shut out the air and sky and turned everything a rusty black. I could think of nothing else but the misery, and it was pointless to try to plan the next move in the game until I rediscovered the ability. It didn't help a bit to know that one more little toot would make me feel just fine again, fix me right up. It especially didn't help to know that there was maybe a million bucks' worth of just the very thing I wanted sealed up in the wall by the bathroom.

So I went out a good deal, in spite of not feeling my best and all, and spent a lot of the next two or three days walking around in the streets. If I stayed around the apartment, that siliconed tile seemed to call out to me whenever I walked past it, or even when I didn't. Away from the house it seemed easier to manage that impulse, so I stayed in the street. I was drinking a good deal, mostly beer, to try to blunt the other symptoms, and whenever I felt too bloated I'd switch over to the mint tea you could get in the Moroccan cafés, where alcohol is forbidden.

It was in one of these tea houses, after a couple of days of this kind of wandering, that I realized that one form of my malaise was giving way to another. I was sitting at a small round table, drinking a long glass of hot sweet tea. Men in djellabas were murmuring at other tables all around me, occasionally giving me short glances of dislike and suspicion (they aren't partial to intruders, on the whole). A cone of sunlight entered the room from a high window and struck an edge of the metalwork tray on my table; the light was sharply, painfully bright. I glanced up, around the room, and it began to ripple from side to side, as though the scene were not real but had been printed on some wild-fluttered fabric. It came to me, the thought ringing in my head like someone else's voice, that it was imperative for me to get back to Racine's immediately before I passed out.

Walking was like a journey up the down escalator. The many steps I felt I was taking did not seem to make me much progress. I was walking up the curl of a great wave made of cobblestones, then as suddenly the street dropped away from beneath me. My head was bobbing like a cork awash and I could hardly feel my arms and legs. Finally I drifted up in front of Racine's door, where it required unreasonable effort for me to operate the key. I stumbled in to my mattress and fell down to sleep.

When I woke up it was night, and looking across the floor from the mattress, I saw that the landscape had stopped swinging up and down. But when I got up, forget it. Racine had come in and fried up a skillet of potatoes and mushrooms, but I wasn't interested. I had some water and went back to bed. And so it went. Sleeping was the only thing I displayed any talent for over the next couple of days. The one good thing about it was that the bug, whatever it might have been, was completely distinct from withdrawal symptoms from the big H, and in fact seemed to displace them altogether.

But it was hard to be grateful even for that. I felt lousy. The big activity of each day was unwinding the bandage off my elbow and giving it the ritual hot soak, and sometimes I was barely up to that. Then it would be stumbling back to bed, nuzzling into the zebra-striped coverlet on the mattress, trying to accustom myself to the new variations in the bob and sway which the room now seemed constantly to maintain. I was flat on my face so often for so long that I got very used to a worm's-eye view across the floor, the texture and details of its surface irregularity, the flocks of dust floating across it.

A couple of days went by like that, and then I got a little better. That's to say, so long as I remained prone or sometimes even propped up on the mattress everything seemed to be stable. But if I rose and tried to walk, the rooms would begin to wiggle again. I didn't venture far from the mattress, and went on sleeping a lot of the time. If wakeful, I read a bit (nothing serious, only a few old Babar and Tintin books that Racine had lying around), or else I worried.

How could Kevin do it? How could he handle such circumstances as these without ending up crawling the walls? It was hard to imagine. The great wondrous secret of Kevin's successes was that he didn't plan anything, or at least that was the conclusion I'd come to. But if he was stuck in a bind like this one — i.e., laid up helplessly sick in a foreign land with a million dollars in the form of nearly raw heroin and with a couple of irritable Bulgarians trailing their automatic weapons around in the shadows by the sickbed — I didn't see how he could survive without planning a little.

Well, maybe it was all just a failure of my perceptions. Or maybe Kevin wouldn't have let his tail get caught in a crack like this to begin with. Maybe he would just leverage someone else into the uncomfortable position. Someone who did plan, like me.

The ability to *delegate* is the mark of a true leader, don't you know.

Of course I mustn't forget that this assignment had originally been delegated to Lauren. Had been set up with her definitely enough in mind that the whole "Anne Morrison" fiction had been laid in on both sides in advance. Well, I could just picture her going through that scene at the no-name café on Rue des Capucins, and when I did it brought the vertigo back, only this time the cause of it was just plain old rage.

Of course it could be argued that I had fouled up the arrangements myself, in a way. "Anne Morrison" might have got a better reception than I did, or at least been received at a better address. Certainly Grushko and Yonko would have been a great deal happier with the contents of that briefcase. So it all might have worked out for the best.

Possibly.

It was getting to be like opening a series of containers within containers, each one concealing a smellier, slightly more unpleasant surprise than the one before. That deliberate exposure of Lauren was almost the nastiest thing of all, so far as I was concerned. But it's part of the character of an infinite recession that the final box is much too small to open or even see. And anyway, there isn't one.

More fool I for not being able to see it coming. You could chalk it up to my being overly involved with my own methodology. Even in the very depths of not thinking about it, I'd always kind of featured it as a coke deal. Or maybe pharmaceuticals, or maybe (outside chance) some change of pace on the order of currency smuggling. Heroin just hadn't entered my mind, despite the fact that from the very beginning we'd had Belgium, and next we had Bulgarians, who live next door to Turkey, where the poppies grow. I knew people had been running scag out of Turkey through Belgium. The reason I knew was they'd been getting caught, which did not make me very happy now, as you may imagine. What kept me from putting it all together before was that I wouldn't have done it. I'd have had no theoretical problem (not much at least) with the idea of shipping coke through Brussels. If I'd got into scag, which I wouldn't have on purpose, I'd probably have tried to bring it in through Colombia.

So this was the first time I'd even met any Bulgarians, and already I didn't like them much. So far I supposed I liked Yonko the least. Grushko seemed a comparatively approachable sort, someone you might be able to really talk to, provided you had a language in common with him, whereas Yonko struck me as your typical trigger-happy juvenile-delinquent street animal, give or take a few cross-cultural variations like that jewelry. Of course that might be the generation gap, or something like the fact that I tend to hate all people who have ever pointed guns in my face. It was not terrifically comforting to think of Yonko and Grushko combing Brussels for traces of me, as they were no doubt doing at this very moment, armed with one or perhaps more machine guns. They hadn't been very inexorable so far, to be sure, and in my moments of semidelirium they even seemed a little funny in some ways, but I knew it would be a risky mistake to mix them up with the cartoon villains in Tintin.

The trouble was that people always got so goddamn serious when it was heroin. Although the distinction was false once you really thought about it, trading in coke always seemed comparatively innocuous, a game of sorts that you could delude yourself was played by rules. In spite of the fact that you could get shot with real bullets and do real time and, of course, make very real money if those more unpleasant kinds of possibilities didn't come to pass. And at least you did deal with a slightly better class of people, on the receiving end anyway. People might try to kill you for a big box of coke, but not for a little syringe full of it, and that, I suppose, made the fine split-hair's worth of difference.

It was not pleasant to think about getting involved in heroin trade, whether by accident or design. What the hell had Kevin really been up to with this movie? I could picture him more clearly now, moving among the junkies and ex-junkies with his usual smoothness, the long easy smile, the charismatic flourishes which must have done a lot to draw those terrible confessions I'd seen in the rushes out of the people who had made them. Again I felt the sprockets engage — forward, reverse, back in slow motion — I saw Kevin juggling all his options, Kevin finishing the shoot itself of course, Kevin setting up his deal with Grushko (who was in there too, right? standing with Kevin just outside the frame), Kevin maneuvering me into position, Kevin making friends with all those junkies . . . Well, that last feature might just have been a singular failure to relate the cause to the effects, not unusual for Kevin, but if he was using them to set up distribution contacts . . .

If so, there might be more people eventually wanting to kill him besides just me.

Bad scene. Again I saw those needles scattered through the rusty brown grass above the Piazza del Popolo, and then looked past that, through that, into all the other needle parks I'd ever wandered through (a tourist, an untouchable) in my time. I remembered faces, not just from the film but the street too: the face of a hundred-dollar habit on its way to one-fifty, two hundred; that look in the eyes; or the face bent over the needle in the swollen vein, in a doorway, any doorway, no thought for exposure anymore, while from other doors along the street you'd hear the dealers calling softly, *Star, star*.

A bad business. No question about that.

Then, just when I thought I had got over the flu or the shipping fever or whatever it had been, it got a whole lot worse and I couldn't worry about anything anymore. I sank through layer after layer of amnesia into what seemed like an endless sleep. How much time was passing I could not have said. I was aware of almost nothing. Vaguely I realized that Racine was around a good deal more than he had been lately, and that he was keeping me supplied with juice and soup and the like, but I didn't have the power to thank him, and sometimes I suspect I didn't know who he was. Staggering to the bathroom, which was the only thing I could get up for, I'd pause and stare at my reflection in the curtained glass pane of the door, would cautiously raise an arm and hand and point out my cloudy features to myself, examining them with hardly any recognition.

Kierkegaard, who suffered from paralytic fits, among other things, used sometimes to fall out in the midst of dinner parties and the like. From the floor he'd call out to his friends, referring to his body, "Oh, leave it till the maid comes in the morning to sweep."

My dreams, of course, were lurid, and in the middle of one I was awakened by a sound hardly more dramatic than the rattle of an electric typewriter, but when I opened my eyes there was a shower of glass all over the room, and Racine was kneeling in the corner with something in his hands. I passed out again, not interested, and the next time I could look around the room I saw the big front window had been partly boarded up. Racine was not going out anymore at all, it seemed to me, except very briefly and hurriedly to the little grocery shop next door, and I also noticed that the sniper rifle had come out of the hole behind the tiles and was now assembled and prominently displayed in the front room.

It was about this time that the drumming began. It was a complicated, constantly changing beat, sometimes accompanied by a kind of chanting, sometimes not. It never stopped; I seemed to hear it even when I slept, and therefore I did not quite believe it was real — I thought it might have been coming out of my own body, from my outraged lungs or heart.

Whether it was real or imagined, inner or outer, I listened to it with some fascination, letting it rock me in and out of the phases of my fever.

And then, one night, I was not sick anymore, as simply as that. I woke up and knew the fever had broken. When I got off the bed the room stayed in one place. I walked over to the boarded window and looked back up at the ceiling, where you could see the pattern of holes from the machine gun burst. A funny sort of angle. It must have been meant for a warning shot. Outside, the drumming continued; it had been real after all. Hungry as a horse, I headed for the kitchen.

Racine was sitting at the table under the light, smoking a cigarette, drinking a Stella. As I entered his hand left the bottle and floated softly to the stock of the little rifle which lay across the table, pointed toward the door.

"*C'est moi, seulement*," I said.

"*Bon*," Racine said. "*Tu vas mieux?*"

"*Ouais*," I said, investigating the refrigerator. There was beer and bread and cheese, all of which I brought over to the table.

"How long have I been out of it?"

"About five days, altogether."

I made a crude sandwich and began to chew.

"I might have had the doctor," Racine said. "Only it seems not such a very convenient time to go out."

"I understand," I said. "I gather we've had visitors."

"*C'est évident.*"

"Once?"

"All that was really possible. There was some difficulty with the police after the first time."

"Not too unpleasant for you, I hope."

"Not so much," Racine said, laughing out of one half of his mouth. "I think they are not very concerned about my health either."

"Well."

"It has its advantages, true. But — "

"I know. It would be nice to be able to walk down to the corner occasionally."

"I agree."

"I think we could get to work on that more or less right away."

"When you feel well enough."

I finished my bread and cheese and took a cigarette from Racine's pack. Outside, the drumming shifted gears and a high wailing began.

"What's with the drums?" I said.

"Haitians."

"I didn't know they had Haitians here," I said. "I thought only the North Africans."

"There are not so many," Racine said. "But they've been there about a year. A block over, on Rue de la Victoire."

"So what are they so excited about?"

"They do the voodoo, I think." Racine pushed away from the table. "No, it's interesting. I heard yesterday, in the store. One of their priests sent a spell against an enemy, and the spell, what would you say, turned back on him."

"Backfired."

"Yes. The Haitians call it *choc en retour*. The enemy turns the spell back on you. So this one got sick. And the people were drumming and singing to try to bring him back again. But they say the spell is reflected back as strongly as it was sent at first."

"So?"

"He died this morning. Now they drum for the funeral."

"It must have been a very bad spell," I said. "And a strong enemy."

"Yes."

"*Choc en retour*. It's an idea, isn't it?"

"They're interesting, the Haitians," Racine said. "They know more than you think."

13

NEXT MORNING I was out of the apartment, for the first time in over a week, walking down Rue d'Irlande, and then crossing over to Rue de la Victoire, where those Haitians were. Although the sky was overcast, the outdoors light was shocking to me, and it felt peculiar to walk too, my out-of-shape tendons creaking whenever I went uphill. I walked south on Rue de la Victoire. Couldn't tell exactly where the Haitians lived. The drumming had stopped the previous night and had not resumed, but I was still thinking about them, still intrigued with the notion of *choc en retour* and its various possible ramifications. The unaccustomed brightness of the open daylight made my eyes run, even behind sunglasses. Every so often I glanced to the side, checking to make sure the blue Peugeot hadn't lost me yet.

Two blocks up the street I went into a bar. There was no one there except for the proprietor and a man with a tight potbelly and slick black hair who was practicing his bumper pool, alone. I ordered a beer and took a table by the window. The coasters on the table had cartoon illustrations printed on them, covering the history of the beer I was drinking, and I began to line the coasters up side by side. Two car doors banged outside, one after the other, and I looked out. Grushko and Yonko were crossing the street. Yonko looked grim, while Grushko seemed merely unhappy. Yonko was wearing a pink tank top, which tended to highlight his least attractive anatomical features. There was a light bandage on his upper arm, but his movement was free enough. Racine had only nicked him, evidently; he'd probably be displeased to hear that. Yonko had given up shaving, I noticed, so maybe he *was* a little sore. His raincoat was wrapped around his right forearm and hand. He'd be in a pretty fix if it rained, wouldn't he? and it did rain a lot in Brussels. One day he was going to drop that package and get himself in a lot of trouble. The two of them walked into the bar and took seats at my table without waiting for an invitation.

I waved to the bartender for two more beers. No one said anything until he'd set the glasses down and gone back to the counter. The Bulgarians didn't touch their glasses. The hell with it, I thought, and tossed off mine. Then I pointed at Yonko's beer and when he didn't react I picked it up and had a belt. It was a clear provocation and at first I didn't understand why I'd done it; it came from some sort of reflex. Then Yonko drew back the folds of his raincoat and thrust the exposed inch of submachine gun muzzle under the table into me. This was the tricky and difficult part, the moment I wanted to get to and past as quickly as possible.

"So shoot me," I said. Yonko was the English speaker, but I was hoping that Grushko might at least pick up the tone. "Shoot me now and you won't get any money and you won't get any dope."

Yonko was leaning out to the edge of his chair, looking more wolfish than ever. His teeth were pointed and blackened in places, I noticed now for the first time, and his breath was not good. He was just a no-account kid, I thought, and I really wouldn't have put it past him to pull the trigger right there in the bar in spite of the witnesses and the difficulty of escape, but I reached down, slowly, no sudden alarming movement, and pushed the gun muzzle off my hip, down toward the tobacco-littered floor. Grushko nodded.

"Get rid of him," I said, indicating Yonko with my thumb. "I need to talk to you alone."

Grushko spoke shortly in Bulgarian and Yonko withdrew to another table deeper in the bar, where he sat down facing us, baleful as ever. The bartender brought him a fresh beer and after a moment he set the rolled raincoat down on an empty chair, picked up his glass and drank from it. I found I was breathing more easily once I saw that, and the knotted muscles in my neck and back began to unwind.

At my table, Grushko leaned forward and began to knead the top of his head, slowly and with great concentration, working around the edges of his bald spot, which began to turn pink under this massage. His fingers were thick and stubby, and on one I noticed he wore a plain gold ring. I waited, finishing Yonko's beer, and after a moment he lifted his head and began to speak.

"My nephew is impulsive," he said. *By cracky, he spoke English after all.* It might be a good omen if disinformation was beginning to work in my favor. Maybe . . . It had not occurred to me that Yonko and Grushko were related, but I supposed that was no more improbable than any other thing. "He has a problem with his self-control. But he is not really a bad boy."

"Yonko, you mean?"

Grushko nodded. It wasn't quite my picture of Yonko, but it wasn't worth arguing about either. Grushko's face, side-lit from the window, was deeply lined around the eyes and mouth. I saw the gray in his crown of hair and realized he had to be ten years older even than me, which put us both a bit past it for this sort of activity.

"All his life he has wanted to live in America," Grushko said. "What he wishes more than anything in the world is to become an American policeman."

I restrained my emotion at learning this interesting fact. And after a moment of reflection the picture of Yonko as, say, a New York City cop seemed much less ridiculous than it had at first.

Grushko rubbed his eyes. "It's very serious for us now, at the moment. Bulgaria is . . . not such a free country. You understand?"

"You can't go back?"

"I am an artist," Grushko said, but in a tone of such little pretension that I took him quite seriously despite the lapses I'd detected in his camera work. "Not well respected by the government of now. And not for many years. My work may be . . . what it may be, but to me it is important. You are an editor and you understand this."

"Oh. You did recognize me, then."

"Of course. And I have seen your work."

I inclined my head, though I thought he was probably fibbing about this last part. Any place he might have seen my cutting, a person wouldn't have been likely to hang around for the credits.

"Your camera work was very fine and it was a pleasure to edit it," I said. Half-truth for half-truth. I was losing track of where this conversation was leading, though Grushko apparently was not.

"Then there is the other matter . . ."

"Our business?" I said.

"Yes. You see . . . ah . . . let me only say that it makes it even harder to return . . . impossible, you see?"

"Burned your bridges." I engaged in the thought experiment of supposing that Jerry Hansen had been armed with a submachine gun when he debarked from the Nova Scotia ferry that day. Well? In one way it made me sympathize with Yonko, and in another way it didn't.

"And we depend very much on the money. You see. Otherwise . . ."

"Yes."

"So." Grushko put his hands palms down on the table and leaned forward onto them.

"You are the friend of Mr. Carter?"

"We've met," I said, sliding my hands down to my knees so that they would not tremble.

"He promised to send someone who would help us through to America."

No fooling? This was getting presumptuous even for Kevin. It wasn't just scag he wanted anymore; I was supposed to start smuggling *people*.

"Not to mention the money?" I said.

"Of course."

"But I can't give you the money . . ."

Grushko sat back. "I let Yonko shoot you then?"

Just when everything was going so nicely, too. I smiled, though I no longer really felt like it.

"What good would that really do you?"

"Maybe in the arm? The leg?"

"No, thank you. Look. There's been a mistake. You saw what was in that bag yourself."

"A mistake?"

I had to admit myself it didn't sound all that convincing, but it was what I had.

"*I* didn't have the combination. That was the setup, wasn't it? I know how it looks. But I'm just the delivery man."

"Then you must give us back our knapsack."

"But then I have my own obligations too, you see, back in America."

"It's not good," Grushko said. He dragged his fingers back across the table and folded his hands in his lap. He really did look pretty worried about everything, which I could hardly blame him for.

"I know," I said. "Look." And I hesitated. I'd thought it all through before this morning, it was almost as if it had been worked out unconsciously in my fever, and yet now it seemed hard to begin to say the necessary words. "We have to solve the problem, don't we? I can't get the money yet, it's impossible, but maybe I can get you to New York. That's part of it, no? Does that help you?"

"You know we need papers."

"Of course," I said, though I really hadn't considered it. "I'll work on it right away."

"To deliver here?" Grushko looked a little happier.

"No," I said, improvising. "In London. In two weeks."

I gave him the telephone number of the flat near Paddington. The landlady would think them peculiar, I knew, but I *had* warned her I needed the place for business.

"It's not what we had hoped," Grushko said.

"I'm sure," I said. "But you would have killed me, wouldn't you? Could you blame me if I'd just disappeared altogether after the last time we met?"

"No," Grushko said. "It's arranged, then,"

"It's arranged," I said, and he pushed back his chair.

"Wait," I said, and for a second it was hard to breathe and I had to gulp before I spoke. "You'll need everything you have here in New York again. *Everything*. You understand?" Grushko nodded and I knew he'd grasped the message. Then I felt what Kevin must have felt sometimes, a shadow of unacknowledged intent welling up behind my eyes and for a moment darkening them, a pulse steadily pounding, like the drums.

Racine solved the immediate technical problem which arose out of all this by introducing me to Clérmont, who seemed to be another hangover from "the old days of *la politique*." Clérmont was a big stooping man, very jovial in manner, with a head shaped like an ostrich egg, which he kept shaved completely bald. Even his eyebrows were shaved and naked. Clérmont had enormous double-jointed hands, which were adept at delicate niggling tasks. He was a graphic designer during the work week, a printmaker by personal vocation, and somewhere in between he was also, well, a forger.

He was a fast and good one too, to the extent of my ability

to judge. One night Racine and I went over to see him, taking along two passport snaps of Yonko and Grushko, along with some other baggage. We sat at one end of Clérmont's long narrow workshop drinking beer and planning the immediate future, while Clérmont himself perched on a high stool over a drafting table in the rear. Clérmont bent low over the papers on the board, working away with his various inks and glues and a couple of little tools that looked like dental picks. His hands made spidery shadows under the high intensity lamp. Every so often he'd smile or mutter something, but he didn't seem to require any reply. It took him two hours, maybe a little longer, to finish, and even as a novice I was impressed with the job; even the embossing looked okay. He'd turned Grushko and Yonko into a couple of Dutchmen. That struck me as a little odd; I'd have had an easier time picturing them as Turks or Hungarians or something. But Dutch passports were what Clérmont had around, and I didn't have any extra passports at all, so Dutchmen is what they had to become.

By the time we were done admiring Clérmont's work it was late, probably after midnight, and time to make the next move. Clérmont was letting us borrow a car for the maneuvers out of town. So I put on a djellaba and a khufi hat I'd brought along in my bag, which were supposed to make me look like a Moroccan. I suppose it might have deceived someone in the dark. Well, however silly I felt, there was no such thing as too careful, and although there'd been no blue Peugeot following us earlier, there might always have been something else. I thought the personal disguise was pushing it, but it hadn't been my idea.

Clérmont helped me load up the car with our bags and the tube that concealed Racine's little rifle and a sizable tin trunk, which was no joke to carry. Then I shook hands with him, standing in the dark under the broken streetlight where he'd had the foresight to park, and then I jumped in and drove off. About ten miles down the road to Ghent I pulled onto the shoulder. There'd been no headlights behind me for ten minutes, and that was good enough for me.

I got out and opened the back door of the car and dragged the trunk down, as gently as I could, until it rested with one end on the pavement. There wasn't a sound from inside it and I grew anxious as I fumbled at the catches. But when I opened the lid I could hear Racine breathing in there, though he didn't say anything at first. After a moment he clambered stiffly out, stumbled, and stood leaning against the car on the shoulder of the road, rubbing at his joints.

"I think we overdid it," I said. And remembering the djellaba, I pulled it off over my head. "There wasn't anything behind us the whole way out of town."

"Probably. But what everyone knows about Clérmont is that no one ever caught him doing anything."

No one had ever caught me either, I reflected then, at least not yet, but I said nothing to Racine on this subject. We remained standing by the car for long enough to smoke a cigarette. A heavy fog had begun to lower over the road, and it roiled across the headlight beams, which I had left turned on. When it began to rain we both got into the car. Racine took the wheel and piloted us around to the north of the city again, to take the road for Antwerp.

"It can be done," Racine had said a few days before, after I'd outlined the difficulties as I perceived them, after we'd agreed that a full partnership was the only way to go from here and were settling down to the details, across his kitchen table. "No, I'm sure, I know the way."

"Let me in on it, then," I said.

"You've never done any diving?"

"Never."

Racine leaned back in his chair, blowing smoke up at the ceiling.

"It's okay, though," he said at last. "Because I have." And

175

that was how the labor was divided; like usual, I had the theory, and this time he had the technique.

The drill for Antwerp was strictly Racine's responsibility, and he decreed that we would see little of the city. We arrived in the dark and he checked us into a waterfront hotel and we scarcely left it again during daylight. Racine went out to procure the Aqualungs and the other gear while I stayed in and studied shipping schedules, my part of the first day's chores. Racine ordered no beer and as few cigarettes as possible, because we were in training now.

So it was a wound-up few days I was in for, though I never completely lost control. Racine found it easy enough to switch to daytime sleeping, but for me it was harder, and I spent many hours of each day standing at the window, staring out at the Schelde River through the slits of the Venetian blinds. What wears people down, as I knew very well, is the boredom of waiting, which can make a person rush out and make a fatal mistake for the sake of doing *something*. Even when I was where I preferred to be, far, far away from the actual transaction, the tension had always told on me, and now it was smoldering, like a fine electric network stippled all over my skin. I didn't get used to it exactly, and it didn't go away, but after a day or so the anxiety lost its negative value and became a sensation I could savor like a drug.

For the first three nights, after darkness had fallen, we left the hotel and Racine drove us to the empty beaches down the coast. On the drive down he'd try to explain parts of it, talking about breathing, about relaxation, while I stared out the window, half listening, at the flat black sea slipping by. It was cold on the beaches, cold sand between my toes, and the air tank was chilly and heavy on my back, but the water itself was freezing, so impossibly cold that I could feel my organs shrinking inside me as I went under.

Down under. The most remarkable thing was the darkness.

Ten feet below, the surface lost its last faint luminescence and I only knew which direction was up by way of my own buoyancy. It was like death, I could imagine, but I was breathing, sucking air from the tank with a ragged throttling sound, incredibly loud, and I could feel the trail of bubbles sifting across the side of my face and up toward the surface. Then Racine's light snapped on and I saw him easily rolling over and gesturing, a true frogman, then swimming away with me after him, following the fading light, the fins on my feet propelling me forward with a good deal more verve than I felt. The first night it was only swimming and breathing and getting used to the long periods underwater. On the second night he started me swimming with some weight strapped to my belt, and on the third the weight was more. Driving back to the city just before the dawn of our fourth day in Antwerp, Racine declared that I was ready, though I myself was not so sure.

On the fourth night we went prowling among the interlinked branches of the Haven, equipped with a Starlite scope with which we could read the lettering on the stern of our ship: the *Eleusis*, a Greek freighter, bound for New York by way of Dover, now moored in Havensdok 2e. We worked back from the *Eleusis* toward the Schelde, measuring angles and estimating times, once flattening ourselves beneath a truck when a port guard passed by.

That was the dress rehearsal, and next was opening night. Racine and I dropped ourselves into the Schelde near the Royersluis canal. There was something to be said for the practice I'd had; I was used to the feel of the water now, though here it was an inky oily black, darker by far than at the beaches. Somewhere ahead Racine's light came dimly on and I churned away after it. I felt competent, unconcerned even by the rubber-swathed package that was bound to my belly like a pregnancy.

But it seemed to be taking a long time. Too long, I thought, though Racine had the watch. He veered to the right (were we through the channel?) and after a little while more, to the left. Another long swim and then a turn to the right, which should have been our last. But Racine stopped and let me catch up. Treading water, he made some odd gestures with his hands, but I couldn't figure out what he was trying to get across. I motioned him on. He shrugged and swam back in the direction we'd come from. I followed, trying to resist the fear: if we were lost we might run out of air, but the more I panicked the faster I'd breathe.

Then Racine stopped and when I reached him he gave the thumbs-up sign. I nodded, and he switched off the light and floated upward. He would take the risk of surfacing for a brief final orientation. We'd decided that earlier, on a toss. I waited, hovering, like a fish holding itself stationary, in the total darkness. The light reappeared and Racine swam ahead. I followed more closely this time, until abruptly we were against a wall of curving steel, the hull of our *Eleusis*.

Then there was a quick flurry against the steel plates, the two of us rushing to secure the magnets and the steel webbing that spanned them, a net across the package. Lighter now, I swam toward the surface while Racine double-checked, my hand stretched out above me counting rivets, *five, ten, fifteen*; at twenty-one my fingers broke the surface and I dove again.

The lamp was already some distance away. I swam and after a while I lost track of our turns. Again it seemed much too long, and my air supply, I noticed, was now in the warning zone. I had no idea at all of how far we'd come, how close to safety. I began counting to myself, *one thousand, two thousand*, as much to calm myself and slow my breathing as to restore my sense of time.

At somewhere around two billion, the light ahead went out, which might have meant either good news or disaster. I stopped swimming and let my body rise. When I broke water I tore off my mask and saw I'd made it; I was in the Schelde, only twenty or thirty yards from where we had gone in. Treading water, I heard Racine bursting out of the river behind my back, and I swam in his direction.

"We did it!" he was calling. There was not much need for caution here.

"We did it!" I shouted back. I swam to him, and we hugged and pounded each other's shoulders, right there in the water. *We did it, we did it,* the words beat in my brain, and I danced in the dirty water, perfectly euphoric, though I knew it was really only half done.

PART IV/

/AVAILABLE
LIGHT

STAY FOR THE OTHER HALF is what the limeys are supposed to say, and I've always thought it was a fine old expression, implying, as it seems to, that the second half can be extended to equal whatever you may have chosen to consume up to the given moment. A sort of eternal flotation of the median. I could hear the line the instant I stepped into the Paddington flat, as plainly as if it really had been spoken by the jolly tar on the label of the half-empty bottle of rum I'd left there roughly a month before.

As the dog returns . . .

It had been a long time since I'd really tied on a good one, I realized, slapping the bottle firmly against my palm as I sank back into one of the greasy armchairs. Though for once I'd hardly thought about it, I hadn't been really drunk in an age, what with the long illness and then the abstinence required for the diving. Now, I discovered I'd had the forethought to refill the ice trays before leaving. The top couple of plastic cups had molded, so I took one from the middle of the stack.

Again it was hot, uncharacteristically hot, in London, and after my first drink I got up and pounded the sashes of the window with the heel of my shoe until the paint loosened up again and I could open it. The air outside, however, was scarcely any cooler than the air within. I refilled my cup and sat down. It was very humid. I drank, more quickly now, and watched dusk begin to darken the edges of the window frame; with nightfall the temperature did seem to drop but only by a fraction. I did not turn on the light, but remained sitting in the darkness until I had finished the bottle. Then the bottle was empty, and yet it seemed to have had no effect.

Curious. My mind remained as clear as a new windowpane. I looked all around the room; everything was shadowy but my eyes had adjusted and there was enough ambient light from the street to make the objects in the room reasonably distinct. After considering for a moment, I stood up. Then the rum asserted itself; I reeled to one side and barely saved myself from falling by flinging one hand out against the wall. My body was drunk as a lord, no question, but there had not been the slightest balm to my brain. A bizarre sensation.

Oh, leave it till the maid comes in the morning to sweep.

I straightened up and went into the bathroom, where I switched on the fluorescent tube over the sink. There was a heavy sweat beading all over my face. I dabbed a finger in it and discovered that it smelt of rum. My eyes were red and itchy. I took off my shirt and splashed my head and upper body with cold water. Afterward I remained leaning on the edge of the sink, staring into my own eyes, tracing the lines of my face. Water ran down the creases and stubble, and soon sweat began to burst out again behind it.

Myself.

Well, this was not the maudlin drunk I'd had on my last night in Rome, nor yet the fit of consuming despair that had followed my visit to the Trevi Fountain. No longer was I on the verge of the void. If I did have a problem, rum couldn't touch it, and in my queer invincible sobriety I felt that perhaps I was instead stumbling toward the solution. A solution, of sorts. Yes. It was possible, likely even, that I was coming into possession of myself, though I was not at all sure that I really wanted the inheritance.

Despair begins with division of the will, says Kierkegaard, and mine was not divided anymore, though I knew the demanding old Dane would not approve of what was happening to me — oh, no. It was not any higher self I was discovering, but the beast within, the reptile living in the glands and the serpentine winding of the spinal cord, its blind unity of purpose. Sweat was pouring out of my forehead and even my eye sockets now, a burning sweat, and my hands had gone white from their grip on the edge of the sink. I was afraid, afraid of myself, and locked in that confrontation with my reflected image, I knew that I must have been so for a very long time.

I washed my face again and went into the outer room, where, with some awkwardness, I let down the bed. Slowly I lowered myself onto the mattress. Though my head was still lucid, I felt drowsy now.

You are a student of theology, I see.

Ethics, really. And in any case I am only an amateur.

I chuckled a little in my doze; that exchange seemed perfectly ridiculous now. An amateur, indeed, I'd been giving myself too much credit. Discomfort at that thought brought me fully awake once more and I remembered abruptly why I had felt it was necessary to get drunk tonight. I switched on a light and sat up in the bed. My bag was on the floor, just within reach, and I rolled over and snatched it by the strap and dragged it up onto the bed with me. The movement gave me a second's worth of vertigo — again, a purely physical sensation. I felt in the side pocket of the bag and found the letter by touch.

A pale blue airmail envelope weighing no more than a Kleenex, addressed in red with the characteristic backward slashes of Lauren's hand. I had been carrying it unopened since Brussels, since the day I had really gone to the post office there. Because there'd been no opportunity really to have a long drink and I strongly felt that I would need one before I opened it.

It might just as well have been a telegram:

Whatever you're doing, stop it and come home. Everything is different now. Everything has changed.

Of course it was a good deal more substantial than the blank sheet I hadn't sent her. And not quite what I'd expected, either. I'd looked for a longer letter, full of equivocation, nothing so brief or so definite. The definiteness in particular ran a tingling finger down my backbone.

Whatever you're doing, stop it . . .

Not bloody likely, of course. But for a moment I let myself imagine it. Could I turn my back, just walk away? I couldn't. I was in. *Come home*, she wrote, only where was that supposed to be? New York? The farm? Wherever I found *her*? It would certainly have required some serious changes to bring that bit about, and I urged myself to be suspicious. I reminded myself that those qualities of endless change, life constructed as a series of moments, belong to the seducer, the betrayer. And still that idea went against the grain and I forgot it, dozing off happily enough, with the letter pressed against my ribs.

The telephone woke me and I struck out for it in the dark, tumbling it with a crash and jangle on the floor. It was Grushko, and after he repeated himself a couple of times my head cleared enough for me to gather that he and his charming nephew were waiting for their new passports at a pub on the King's Road.

I hung up and, blearily, checked my watch. There was an hour and a half before closing time. At least I was mostly dressed already. I washed my face and slipped the passports into my inside jacket pocket and went down the stairs. My landlady was standing behind the desk, apparently in a chatty mood.

"And was it the foreign gentlemen, then?" she said. The call had come through her switchboard, which was the only way a call could come.

"I suppose," I said, not really listening, headed for the door. Then it registered and I stopped.

"Which foreign gentlemen?"

"Why, the ones who came round the day before yesterday," the landlady said cheerily.

"For me?"

"Yes, to be sure. But they only stayed a moment and wouldn't leave a message. You were away," she added, a little super-fluously.

"I see." I thought for a second and then went down to the street. God bless the old lady for a Nosy Parker; she just might have saved my neck. There were no loiterers near the building, but I walked all the way around the block to make sure. It was easy enough to spot my second floor apartment in the rear, since I had the only open window. The brick facing of the wall below was rough and an agile person might have been able to climb it without much difficulty. Of course there hadn't quite been time for that, yet. I wound my arms in fast little circles, loosening up — my elbow had healed pretty well by then, and a good thing too — and then went back inside. The landlady, conveniently, was engaged in the rear, so I could dart in and out to retrieve my bag without her knowing any-thing about it.

Time was really a factor now, so I caught a cab and had the driver wait outside Paddington Station while I went in to drop my bag in the cloakroom. Maybe they'd put it next to the package, or maybe they would not. I had the driver wait again in the King's Road, outside the pub, which was, appro-priately enough, called the Lion's Mouth. There was no sign of Grushko or Yonko in the main room and for a moment I almost panicked, thinking I'd miscalculated the whole play. I wandered around the edge of the bar and found a staircase which led down to a game room. Downstairs there were several pool tables and one billiard table. Grushko was deeply engrossed in a game of billiards with a younger man, a punker with spiky hair — so involved he did not notice my arrival, as a matter of fact. Yonko was not in evidence, not much to my surprise. I sat down on a bench and lit a cigarette. Again the time was beginning to matter, but Grushko finished his game before I was done with my smoke. He was starting for the stairs when I stood up to greet him.

"*Bien, bien,*" he said. "You're here at last. A drink?"

We went together up the stairs; I let him lead. On the main floor he started for the bar, but I caught him by the elbow.

"No time for that, I'm afraid," I said. Grushko's smile became distinctly uneasy.

"But I must pay you a beer," he said. "You paid last time, in Brussels."

Not terrifically convincing. My theory was looking better every minute.

"I haven't got the papers here, you see," I said. "We have to go back to my place so I can get them for you."

"No, no, but we must wait for Yonko," Grushko said. "He had to go out for a moment, you see. He will not be back for twenty minutes, a half hour . . ."

"A pity," I said, tightening my grip on his elbow. "But I'm afraid you'll have to catch up with him later. I have a taxi waiting for us just outside the door."

It didn't turn out to be my most amusing cab ride. Even the driver was sullen because I'd made him wait so long. It would have been a little impolitic for Grushko and me to have had much conversation, even if there had been no other cause for tension. A deadly silence fell and endured for the five or ten minutes of the trip. I had the driver stop a good block and a half from my building, and improved his mood slightly by overtipping him.

Grushko was no happier, but perhaps resigned; he seemed stolid enough, at any rate, as we walked down the street.

"Worried about Yonko?" I said, to needle him a little. "Don't fret, I'm sure you'll find each other again soon enough."

"Yes, yes," Grushko said. "No doubt."

I escorted him up the pair of steps to the glass door of the lobby. For the second time that evening the luck of circumstances stuck with me; the landlady was not at the counter. The hum and glow of her little black-and-white television issued through the crack of the door behind the desk, but she herself did not appear in the few seconds it took us to reach the stairs. In the stairwell, Grushko hesitated; he was listening for something, apparently enough. Again, I took him by the elbow and urged him on, keeping a comfortable half step behind.

Walking into the hallway turned out to be the rough spot I hadn't anticipated, the place where I almost blew it, blinded by overconfidence and the rising excitement of action. It was a good thing I'd kept Grushko a pace ahead of me, because I could see in the tensing and relaxing of his shoulders the preparation for making some sort of major noise. He might have been planning some too-loud piece of conversation, or maybe a real shout that would have completely obliterated the nervous amenities we'd maintained up to then, but he never got a chance to do either. I fell in behind him and jammed my thumbs up under the back of his jaw on either side, blocking the big veins there, stopping him cold. The casual ease with which I slipped into this brutality surprised me a little. I noticed, distantly, that he was exactly a head shorter than I, so that his bald spot fit neatly under my chin.

I edged him forward to the door. To reach my key I had to let go with one hand, but the pulse of the artery kept him immobilized for that extra beat I needed for the lock. Then it didn't matter anymore because it was all starting to happen and I was doing everything by reflex, *door open, light switch*, keeping Grushko in front of me as a shield. Over his shoulder

I saw Yonko whirling around in the area of the bed, holding only a flashlight though. I suppose the machine gun hadn't fit into his cat-burglar routine, and I was grateful for that.

Though he hadn't had all the time they'd bargained for, the time I should have spent hoisting a few with Grushko at the Lion's Mouth, Yonko had done an impressive job on the place. He'd slit the chair cushions and the mattress and torn a lot of paneling down from the walls and even begun on the hollow spots behind the bathroom tiles. Of course it was later that I totaled up the damage, because at that instant I just barely had time to register that Yonko for once, wasn't carrying. I shoved Grushko out of the way — his circulation was still enough impaired that it would take him a few minutes to become a factor in whatever was going to occur — and bent my knees. Yonko was coming at me, and I could sense his confidence in his superior height and reach. It was a pure animal response, but there was plenty of raw hate in his face also, and did I imagine it or was there a flash of recognition too? There was little time to imagine anything, though, no time for the subjective qualities of the experience, because although Yonko seemed to be moving rather slowly I already had to take a step back to make room for the side kick, setting my heel against the doorsill. That always tends to surprise people without training — they see you backing up and then you've hit them. It was either an inspired technique or just a very lucky one. I hit him just under the sternum and he sailed backward over the wreckage of the bed and collapsed into the cabinet behind it, like a vampire sinking back into its coffin.

I stayed poised on the balls of my feet, but Yonko, though conscious, was off the count for now. Grushko had caught his breath but wasn't taking any action, and before he could, I took the two Dutch passports out of my pocket and put them in his hand. That gesture changed the tone of the proceeding, indicating that we were all still in business together despite the recent misunderstanding, et cetera.

Yonko pulled his arms and legs together and sat up in the pile of puffy cotton he'd reduced my mattress to. Still vibrating, I took a step toward him.

"Listen to me," I said, not just for him but for Grushko too. "Go ahead and hate. You've got the right. I don't blame you a bit." There was no calculation at all in what I was saying, it was all just coming out. I could feel that I had Yonko's attention.

"But I'm not the one," I said. "It was never me. It's —" and then I knew I'd already said enough. I too had moved into the pulse of change, reached the moment where the wish and the act are one.

"You know who's responsible," I said, thinking, *ah, so that's how it's done.*

17

ALTHOUGH FLYING TO EUROPE takes all night, when you fly back from Europe you get there only three hours after you left, which was convenient for me this time, since the predeparture period had been more frantic than usual. I had scarcely had a chance to make up with Grushko and Yonko when a knock came on the door, followed by the voice of my landlady. Someone adjacent had called to complain of noise, presumably the sound of Yonko slamming into the wall, for there hadn't really been much else. Through the locked door I tried to convince her that I'd only let the bed down a little hastily. After I'd assured her several times that there'd be no further disturbance, she relented and went away.

I got rid of Grushko and Yonko fairly swiftly after that. However confused and irritated they might have been, even they could agree that there was not much use in their hanging around at that moment. They had their Dutch passports, anyway, and I told them they'd have to be satisfied with that and a street corner meet somewhere in New York in a couple of days. I gave them about a fifteen-minute lead out of the place, spending the dead time reckoning up the damage Yonko had done to the flat. The landlady was going to be very disappointed in me, though I did leave her most of my ready cash by way of reparation. It was late enough for her to have gone to bed by the time I crept away myself. I walked to Paddington to collect my gear and from there caught a cab for Heathrow. I had to sit up for the rest of the night, waiting for a flight that would land me in New York around ten the next morning, U.S. time. That left me plenty of time to catch up with the mail.

Homeward bound. Lauren's letter was filed away for the moment. Who I had to think about was Kevin. I was thinking of him in terms of S.K.'s mystical question: Did he laugh when he was alone? If he was laughing, somewhere in secret, I hoped to have him laughing out of the other side of his mouth before long. But I did not really think he would be laughing. In a sense the question was not applicable to Kevin, who stood outside the whole issue in an area where the twin-ship of desire and its object is the rule for all action. You have to perceive an irony before it becomes amusing. How does one laugh without reflection? It was just me again, trying to reanimate Kevin by breathing interpretations into him.

And in spite of all that, I was really sort of looking forward to the whole thing. It wasn't just the old affection, so difficult to completely destroy, or the thrill of the mostly fraternal rivalry there'd been between us from the very beginning. I thought now of how I myself had changed, taken a long step in his direction, and I wondered whether he would be able to notice and appreciate that. That really was a vexed question, not a rhetorical one, and my speculation was that he would not, unless across some subconscious synapse — Symparanekro-menoi, the fellowship of buried lives.

I slept then for an hour or so, and when I woke the plane had already caught up with the sun. It was going to be a hell of a long day. I still felt stunned, waterlogged with sleep, when the plane landed. Customs was uneventful, though slow.

I gave the cab driver the Brooklyn address and then changed my mind when we hit the expressway. It dawned on me that it would be better to keep a lower profile than that, given all the circumstances surrounding this particular trip. I had the driver take me to the old Earle Hotel. After I checked in there was nothing left to do but try to stay up long enough to straighten out my schedule. I managed to make it until just after dark.

I woke up far and away too early, of course, and had to sit around for a couple of hours waiting for it to get light. I went down to an all-night coffee shop and got a double-large cup to go, then brought it back to my room, where I sat staring out the open window with my feet propped up on the sill. The air outside was cool and damp; the summer was winding down. I'd been gone a long time. As it got lighter, I could see into the north corner of Washington Square. The trees and grass looked lush and green, and I kept studying them as if they mattered to me somehow. Still I was surprised when Grushko and Yonko strolled into the circle of benches around nine o'clock; I'd nearly forgotten I'd promised to meet them there.

It seemed as if some sort of role reversal had occurred when I went down. Yonko looked cheerier than I'd ever seen him, while Grushko looked very stern. Of course, Yonko had always wanted to come to the States, right? He'd already bought himself an "I Love New York" T-shirt. It became him so well that I almost didn't notice that he had that same old raincoat shoved down in a small shopping bag, and that the bag swung more heavily than any raincoat could really account for.

And then I noticed that Grushko had a heavy shopping bag also, which he was carrying in the manner one might handle a basket of rattlesnakes. That seemed to raise the situation to a whole new level of seriousness. I had no idea how they'd made these arrangements, but it seemed certain enough that they had been made. Two for the price of one, oh boy. Of course I had invited them, in a sense. I took a seat between them on the curving bench.

"Well?" Grushko said. He really did seem edgy. He was looking at me sidelong, not even turning his head my way, and he kept fingering his shopping bag in a way that made me sort of uncomfortable. The Pink Pussycat, said the bag. Sure.

"Relax," I said. "You're making me nervous."

"This situation has gone long enough," Grushko said. "We get tired of waiting."

"Well, it's good practice if Yonko really wants to be a cop," I said. "You need a lot of patience for that. Stakeouts and everything."

No one seemed to think that was too funny at all. I guess I should have known better.

"It's time for something to happen," Grushko said.

"I know, I know. But you've really got to be patient for just a few more days. Remember, the business isn't with me. You've got to wait until I make the transfer."

"We'd like to be there," Grushko said flatly.

"That's impossible. You know that."

"Nearby, then."

"Okay," I said, and then I thought for a moment before I went on. But all I could think was that it did all seem to be happening. They were making the moves I needed them to make, without my even having to nudge them. My last little moral holdout was that I wasn't going to give them the *what*, but I did come across with the when and where.

Then for the next little while there was not very much to do except sit around. I procured a shipping list from which I learned that the *Eleusis* would not be in for four or five more days, and until that happened I wouldn't even know whether the whole skin-diving maneuver had done anything more than create a whole new class of junkie whales and sharks. It was time to sit and wait. The most trivial social encounter remained for the moment inadvisable. I'd made a promise to myself that I would stay away from Lauren until the business matters were resolved. The one person I did need to see was Kevin, and for the first day or so I didn't really feel up to that.

But it got awfully boring. I went out some, of course; I had to, but I tried to hold it to a minimum. The only time you have accidental encounters with people you know in New York is when you don't want to. Then also, whenever I did go out, be it only for a cup of coffee or a paper, either Grushko or Yonko appeared on my tail. Always one and never both, which I gathered meant they were keeping the hotel under twenty-four-hour surveillance — a bit excessive, I would have said. It didn't take me long to notice all this, since they made no effort at all to conceal themselves, and I'm sure they wanted me to know they were keeping an eye on me. It didn't matter much. I didn't need my privacy for anything yet, but it was a macabre effect. I spent most of my time in my room. The circumstances were ideal for a total surrender to jet lag. I slept most of the days and spent the nights watching late movies on TV. It might have been a combination of ennui and my weird sleep schedule that finally led me to conceive a sort of novel way for getting in touch with Kevin.

I suppose it goes with the rest of my personality that I am the sort who will never throw away a key. Like a pack rat, or a magpie. Thus my New York key ring is still the size of my fist even though I don't really live there anymore. One night, during a long commercial break on Channel 7, I tried amusing myself by flipping through the keys and trying to remember what doors they used to open. When I hit the set that used to go with Chameleon International Filmworks, the light bulb went on.

I don't throw away keys, and Kevin likes to rotate cylinders.

It was a half-baked idea, but even if it didn't work, which it probably wouldn't, it would at least break the monotony for an hour or so.

It wasn't so late, not much past ten. Yonko was on duty outside the Earle and he fell in behind me as I went up the street. No skin off my nose; Kevin was probably the only person in the world I didn't at all mind leading him to. But once I got into Chelsea I began to feel enough uncertainty to make me hesitate. I went into a Puerto Rican bar on Ninth Avenue where I knew I could knock back a couple with perfect anonymity. There was next to no light, and Yonko, who came in and sat near the door, was probably more conspicuous than I was down in the shadows at the far end of the counter. I had a beer and a shot and a beer and a shot and a beer and a shot, and by the time I left, a little past eleven, I didn't feel uncertain anymore.

Yonko stopped when he saw me go up to Kevin's entryway. I was tempted to wave back at him, but I didn't. Of course the first hitch in the whole scheme was that I had no way of getting past the downstairs door. I'd thought of nothing to cover that contingency, but now, on the spur of the moment, I just mashed all the buttons on the buzzer plate *except* for Kevin's. In a building that size, somebody's always expecting someone. Sure enough, in a second or so here came the buzz.

Upstairs, it all began to seem like an exercise, a true time waster. Kevin's door had a Fox lock set in its center, with the cylinder behind a steel plate where I couldn't read the brand. It no longer seemed a likely proposition, but since I was there I thought I might as well go through the motions. I had six keys from the Chameleon days, three Segals and three Medecos, and I started trying them, quietly, very quietly. The Segals wouldn't go in at all. The first Medeco made it about halfway. The second was a perfect fit. Slowly, softly, I turned the lock.

The door swung into the little end of the ell of Kevin's loft, so that the main living area was around the corner from where I was standing. The lights were on over there and I could just see the beginning of his rows of stills along the white wall opposite. I let the door drift shut, not locking it, and padded toward the light. I was wearing soft-soled tai chi slippers and my feet seemed to make no noise at all on the floor.

It was a straight shot from the corner to the round white table below the windows in back. Kevin was sitting down there. He was facing across the table, in profile to me, and he seemed to have noticed nothing. On the other side of the table sat Lauren.

Freeze frame.

Slammed back into editorial detachment, I studied the tableau down there at the little end of the room. Lauren, I saw, was dressed for the street. She had her shoes on and her purse was near her on the table and she did not have the air of a woman who is, however temporarily, *at home*. It was possible, then, that she had only dropped in for the evening. She was smoking with the fast jerky movements which usually implied that something fairly serious was up. Kevin was watching her closely, leaning a little toward her across the table. After a long, long moment, he sat back in his chair and his eyes drifted up toward the ceiling. It was a classic Kevin vague-out; I could recognize it from the other end of the room. Lauren snubbed out her cigarette and turned toward the windows behind.

My heart faltered. The windows were black, reflective, but if she saw me she gave no sign of it. I detached myself from the wall and walked quietly, deliberately, down the middle of the floor toward the table, watching not the two of them now but the reflections of all three of us. I floated toward our images as if I were riding a dolly. The reflections were dim, a little distorted, unrealized, resembling not the ghosts of the dead but shades, perhaps, of the as yet unborn. It was passing strange that no one had noticed me yet. I reached the table and stopped beside it, and after a moment I let my knuckles fall and click against the Formica top.

There we are.

Kevin swiveled in his chair and looked at me, eyes blurry, with no real sign of recognition. Lauren was more composed and I realized she probably had been watching my approach after all. She rose, apparently with perfect calm, and slung the strap of her purse over her shoulder.

"I've got to go," she said to Kevin, who nodded but did not otherwise respond. Lauren came round the table to me and kissed me on the cheek. A tremble of her fingers against my collarbone.

"Come see me," she said. "I'm at Christine's. Come soon." The tremble turned into a squeeze for emphasis, and when she met my eyes I blinked. Her heels clicked across the floor and she was gone.

"I let myself in," I said to Kevin. "Hope you don't mind." I sat down in the chair where Lauren had been.

"What?" Kevin said.

I looked at him. He was still a long way away, and I wondered what they might have been talking about, though I guessed I'd probably never know for sure. I lit a cigarette and held it, watching the plume of blue smoke waver between us. Lauren's ashtray, I saw, was full. Kevin rubbed his eyes and yawned like a cat.

"So you're finally back," he said. I had his attention now. Finally there was somebody home behind his eyes, which I noticed were rimmed with black. Kevin looked tired, and for the first time ever I thought he looked old too. All over his head his hair was beginning to fleck with white, and though naturally that wouldn't have caused it, I remembered that he would have been under some stress and strain himself these last few weeks, especially if he'd borrowed money. All that money.

"Your movie was a mess, man," I said.

"I guess you fixed it, though. That's what we're paid for, right?"

"That's what we're paid for," I said, then idly repeating it: "That's what we're paid for here."

"It went okay?"

There was a note of anxiety in his voice that I didn't catch at first because I was thinking about the film again, as is my way.

"I had to throw about half of it out," I said. "You know how I feel about available light. It was practically coming out black in places."

"Oh, the film," Kevin said. "I talked to Dario. He's very happy with the cut."

"*Bene, bene,*" I said.

Kevin laughed, dropping back for a moment into his old charm.

"He's a flit, isn't he?" Kevin reached across the table and without thinking I shook his hand. The touch came like an electric shock, followed by a convulsive surge of darkness. Again I was struck by the uncanny resemblance we sometimes had to one another . . . and the bond. *Darkness made flesh.* Would I look so to him? Briefly I hoped that it wasn't going to happen, that it could all be deferred somehow. I dropped his hand.

"And that gonzo Bulgarian cameraman . . ." Kevin was still chuckling.

"Yeah," I said. "Him too."

"So," Kevin said, becoming serious again. I felt the curtain drop back between us. "How did it go?"

"It went," I said.

"You don't know how glad I am to hear that," Kevin said. "It's been a little humid around this town lately. I couldn't tell where you were or anything. I didn't know what was happening."

"No kidding?" I said. "Neither did I."

Kevin caught my tone enough to look slightly uncomfortable. I have to give him credit for that much.

"I didn't want to get overextended," he said.

I let that one sit a minute.

"Or you either, of course," Kevin said, squirming a bit, I thought.

"Or Lauren," I said.

Kevin shifted around in his chair. "She's been back for a while, hasn't she?" he said. "I didn't know. She just dropped in tonight. Didn't call or anything, just rang the bell downstairs."

Kevin was really wriggling now, I sensed. He'd never been much good at all at outright lying. It was strange because I couldn't understand why he was taking the trouble.

"She'd only been here about a half hour," he said.

"So forthcoming, Kevin," I said. "You feeling okay tonight?"

Kevin smiled and again I got the flash. *Recognition*. A point. Whose?

"It's been kind of dicey around here, like I told you," Kevin said. "I didn't quite know what to tell my partners. Still don't as a matter of fact."

"Gee," I said. "And I don't even know who they are or anything."

"Oh well," Kevin said. "What would really be the good of that? I mean, as long as you're satisfied with your piece?"

Hard to believe. Even though I had expected it.

"Considering the magnitude and all," I said, very slowly, "I think my end might go up a little."

"Sure," Kevin said quickly, though he looked definitely worried. Of course he'd have no idea I'd opened that briefcase. "We'll work something out . . ."

"Was this how you got so interested in drug rehab, Kevin?"

"Now, now. I'm *sure* you don't really need to know about that end of it."

"Just idle curiosity," I said. "But you know, there hasn't been a whole huge amount of freedom of information anywhere on this deal. That can cause a person some problems, you know what I mean? It was a bit dicey at my end too."

"Ah, but I knew you'd come through, Tracy. You always do."

"Yeah," I said. "I always come through."

"I guess you didn't bring it tonight, though?"

"Not yet," I said. "I need . . . three more days."

"Why so long?"

"Remember, dear. What you don't know won't hurt you?"

"All right, then. You'll bring it here?"

"No. You'll have to pick it up."

"Where?"

"The bridge."

"Bridge? What bridge?"

"The one to my place. Around the middle of the walkway up there. At one A.M., let's say."

"Jesus. It's a little theatrical, don't you think? Does it really have to be there?"

"If you want to get your package it does."

"Okay, okay. You're not mad at me or anything, are you? Did you really have such a tough time over there?"

"I'm not mad at you," I said, surprised to find that this was true. I wasn't angry, only cold. "It was interesting. I learned a lot."

"Like what?"

"Voodoo."

"Voodoo? Like sticking pins in dolls?"

Like reaping the whirlwind.

"All in due time," I said. "There's a time and a place for everything."

Kevin yawned.

"You're right about that," he said. "I think it's time for me to get some sleep. I've been having trouble lately. But now you're back . . ."

We both stood up.

"What's it all going toward?" I said. "By the way."

"Oh, nothing particular. General expenses. Why?"

"There's a rumor going around you're starting a feature."

"No. Completely false. It would be nice, of course. But I really don't think I'm ready."

Lauren would be thrilled to hear that, I thought.

"Oh yeah," Kevin said, coming around the table to walk me toward the door. "Lauren."

Like he'd read her name right off my mind.

"What about her?"

"I just wanted to . . . to wish you good luck. Both of you. Together. I'd like to see things work out."

"You would?"

"Well, maybe there've been some problems," Kevin said, tapping his hand against my shoulder. "I won't say I totally didn't have anything to do with them if there were. But you know. Situations change."

Suitably equivocal, that was. We'd reached the door.

"If you say so," I said. I really didn't know what to make of any of this. I pulled the door open and stepped into the hall.

"So," Kevin said. "Best wishes always. That's all I meant."

"Was it?" I said. I could feel that I was gaping at him. "Well, thanks a lot."

"Good night, then," Kevin said. "See you in a couple of days." And he smiled and shut the door in my face. I stood there for a moment, goggling at the keyhole, and then I went on down the stairs.

The lights on 19th Street hadn't been repaired yet, but though I remembered the mugging attempt with perfect clarity, I didn't hurry. I had Yonko to watch my back this time, after all, and there seemed to be something suitable about walking in the dark. Kevin had thrown me another loop with that parting line, though I didn't think it really affected the basic paradigm. The machinery was in motion anyway and it would do what it would do.

It was out of my control. I had my own secret now, my

own webwork of seduction. Necessity had brought me to it, or so I believed, and I believed also that the secret was wrapped up in love and not only in fear, though I couldn't tell for sure, because the whole point was that it was secret from me too. The flower of love grows out of the deep fearful night, or that's what S.K. says, anyway. I'd made the movements well enough that I honestly no longer knew exactly what I was doing, but there on the silent street I had a premonitory glimmer of just how fearful that night could turn out to be. Enough that I had to hope I wasn't making a mistake. There was no way of knowing absolutely if the scales had fallen from my eyes or onto them. There was no light available to me now; I was on my own in the dark.

18

ON MY WAY BACK to the Earle I
stopped by the late night liquor store on 14th Street and bought
myself a pint of something to settle my stomach and quiet my
nerves and help me get to sleep and everything. In my room
I sat up for most of the rest of the night, drinking bourbon
and tap water and watching a series of vampire movies on TV.
I was getting TVed to death, and the bed was starting to look
and feel like an ashtray. When the set finally collapsed into
white noise, I just rolled over and went to sleep.

When I finally woke up the news was on, the six o'clock
evening news, that is. I was becoming a real nightbird, but at
least it did suit my situation. I had a shower and got dressed.
Took a look at the bottle and decided I'd better let it alone. I
went out. Grushko was on point downstairs. He trailed me to
a bank of phone booths on Sixth Avenue. I didn't think the
Bulgarians really would have had the connections or ability to
tap my line at the hotel, but they'd surprised me a time or
two already and I didn't want to take any chances.

I got lucky. Lauren was home and willing to stay there until
I could come by, which I told her was going to depend on
circumstances. These circumstances involved the evasive ac-

tion I would need to devise to shake off Grushko, though naturally I didn't tell her that.

I hung up and went farther west, heading for Seventh Avenue, with Grushko keeping a precise half block behind me. Whenever I glanced back at him I saw the Pink Pussycat shopping bag swinging at the full length of his arm, like the pendulum of a clock. I was just never going to get used to that part, but Lord willing it would all be over in a couple more days.

Grushko almost missed the light crossing Seventh. Almost, not quite. He got back in position as I went down Barrow Street. After a little way I turned onto Bedford and then went into Cholmondeley's.

It was cocktail time in the West Village and I got the last free stool at the bar. Grushko had to take a table and he didn't look very happy about it. Probably they were having cash flow problems, I thought, but I wasn't going to feel guilty over it; I'd never asked them to follow me everywhere I went. I ordered a piña colada because I don't like piña coladas. I wanted to stay perfectly straight for Lauren, who generally preferred me that way. The drink came and I looked at it until Grushko was served his beer. Then I got up and strolled in the direction of the bathrooms around the corner in the rear. Cholmondeley's is one of the few New York bars I know of that has a back door, and after crossing a small courtyard I was back on Barrow Street. I jogged to the corner, made a right, jogged to the next one and made a left. A couple of people turned their heads as I went by but none of them was Grushko. I slowed to a walk. No pursuit. Back on Seventh Avenue, I caught the subway for deepest darkest Tribeca.

Christine's place, a loft in a commercial building on Duane Street, had formerly been Lauren's own place, back in the days of yore around the time she had her stroke. I hadn't been there much since those times, and when she buzzed me in I was struck by how long and steep that staircase to her third floor landing really was. I went up slowly, and when I reached her floor I turned and looked back down. It was quite some rough-and-tumble distance down the metal stairs to the steel street door. *Yeah*, I thought to myself, *it probably would have worked*.

"What are you staring at?" Lauren said lightly. She'd opened the door behind me and I hadn't noticed.

"Oh, nothing, dear, nothing at all."

"Well, come in, then," she said, and turned away from the door. I followed her, looking down at her heels moving along the floor; her feet were wet and were leaving damp prints behind them on the wood. She'd just come out of the shower, I gathered. She wore a full red robe and her hair was also damp.

In a corner at the front of the main space there were a couple of armchairs, a low coffee table and a couch, on which last I sat down. Lauren remained standing, one hand cocked on her hip.

"I'm having tea," she said. "Would you like some?"

"Sure," I said. "Gladly."

"There's whiskey too if you'd rather," she said with a half smile.

"Tea," I said. "I never take anything stronger than weak tea and dog biscuits." But I didn't get any laugh for that one, only a quizzical look.

"Just a minute," Lauren said, and she walked around the white wallboard box that served as a bedroom and disappeared into the kitchen alcove on the other side of it. I looked around; the loft was remarkably bare. The carpets and the plants were gone and I could see pale patches on the walls where pictures had evidently been removed. I leaned back, resting my head on the plush roll of the back of the sofa. The windows in the place were high, too high to see out of from a sitting position, though they let in a lot of light in the daytime, I recalled. Now the windows were fading from blue to black and what light there was came from track fixtures on the ceiling.

After a minute I heard the kettle begin to whistle and soon

after that Lauren came back, awkwardly clutching two mugs of tea, a pack of cigarettes, and a silver-backed hair brush. I got up to help her but she shrugged me away and carefully lowered the whole cluster to the table. Then she sat down on one of the armchairs, drawing her knees up. I tasted my tea. Hot.

"I must look like a wet rat," Lauren said.

"You look lovely," I said, meaning it. "You always do." Lauren seemed to blush a little, to my considerable surprise.

"From the way you sounded on the phone I didn't expect you quite so soon," she said.

"Things cleared up a little faster than I thought they would," I said.

"Mysterious, aren't we?"

"If you say so." I reached for Lauren's box of Marlboros, took one out and lit it. Lauren leaned forward to pick up the hair brush and went to work with it. Her hair was long and very thick. She lifted cords of it away from her head and with a distant expression on her face began to brush them slowly smooth. I watched for a minute and then, balancing my cigarette on its filter on the table, I walked around behind her chair and took the brush from her hand. The silver backing was dented and worn and I remembered that Lauren's mother had given the brush to her when she married. Precisely, when she married me. I lifted a tress of her hair, heavy with dampness now, and began to brush it out.

"Ah," Lauren said. "That feels so nice."

"It's been a while, hasn't it?" It had always been something I used to do during the good times. Lauren sighed but said nothing more articulate, and I went on brushing her hair, from the roots to the ends, until it was completely soft and dry. I have no idea how long it took because I was half hypnotized. At length I set the brush down on the arm of the chair and sank my fingers into the muscles of her neck. Briefly, Lauren rested against me as I rubbed, then she leaned forward and broke my grip.

"Sit down," she said. "I need you over there where I can see you."

Reluctantly enough I lifted my hands from her shoulders and walked back to resume my place on the couch. My cigarette had burned itself out and I picked up the nub and dropped it in an ashtray.

"If there's a wasp in the room you want to see it?" I said.

"That isn't it. That isn't it at all."

"So how do I look?"

"Tracy. Did you get my letter?"

"I got it," I said. "I carried it around for a while. It wasn't till a couple of days ago that I opened it."

"Why?"

"I was afraid to."

It was a novelty, and not an entirely unpleasant one, to find myself telling so much of the truth like that.

"Afraid of what?"

"Of some kind of elegant brush-off."

"Then I hope it was a nice surprise for you."

"Yes," I said. "It was."

"Would it have made a difference? If you'd read the letter earlier. Would you have come straight back?"

"Lauren," I said. "I might as well tell you, I'm fairly deep in the mascara with Kevin at this point, in case you haven't figured that out already. I mean, it's turned out even more unpleasant than it looked when we were in Rome. And —"

"And that was when *you* told *me* to walk away from it all."

"Kevin was using you as a cat's paw and you could have gotten yourself killed."

"And you? You're immortal nowadays?"

"So far," I said, and gave her a weak sort of smile.

"It's not funny," Lauren said, looking truly unamused. "Not if things are as serious as you say."

"It's pretty serious. Very serious, in fact. But you don't have to be in it at all. It's me and Kevin, basically."

"Oh, *basically*," Lauren said. Her face drew in for a second in white lines around her mouth. *"Basically*, it's just you and Kevin, like it always has been."

"Well, it's a nasty little piece of business after all," I said. Now I was confused enough to start to be angry too. "I don't quite understand why you feel such a compelling desire to get involved in it, or get me uninvolved in it, or whatever it is that you want."

"Because I'm your wife."

Oh, that.

"Technically speaking," I said. "If you assume rights you assume obligations too." We were on familiar debating ground now and that was a line that had usually shut her up in the past.

"Exactly," Lauren said. "I'm assuming my obligation to help you get out of this bloody mess."

Startling, that was. But the habit of being abandoned to my own devices whenever the going got tense was too old to be broken so quickly, and I was already shaking my head no.

"It's too late. It's too late for that now, I'm afraid."

"You're both of you so stubborn. Can't you make up your minds to get along or else stay away from each other?"

"We've tried it, you know. Tried both of those things. And anyway, don't you and I sort of have the same problem? And maybe you and Kevin too?"

Lauren took a cigarette from the pack on the table and held it unlit between her fingers.

"You've been seeing a lot of him lately, haven't you," I said, following my hunch.

"Well. There was Florence, first, in April."

"Florence?"

I see the chicken!

"Yes. I didn't . . . I wasn't . . . I suppose I let you think I'd come from New York when I showed up in Rome. I hadn't. I'd been in Florence with Kevin and he went to Paris with me because I was doing a show and then I flew to Rome from there."

"Oh, Christ. You did carry that bag across a few borders, then."

"I didn't know what was in it. I was telling the truth about that. And I suppose you won't tell me, if you know now."

"You're right about that."

"And I have been seeing him some, a lot really, since I came back here. Oh, I know I shouldn't have, with whatever you're into with him going on, I know that. But I didn't get any answer to my letter, and I thought he might drop something about you — oh, don't worry, I didn't ask. And I had my own questions besides."

"Get any answers?"

"Tracy, I do want to tell you the whole truth about this now. If there is any whole truth . . . I never left you for Kevin, I think you know that, but he was very sweet to me when I first got back to New York, before Italy I mean, and I don't know, you know how nice he can be —"

"Sure I do." I did, too.

"And I needed it, then. That was important. That was why I felt like . . . I owed him the favor with the bag. More than the part in the picture or anything like that. And before I came to Rome I was still very angry at you."

"Okay," I said.

"But after Rome I wasn't angry anymore and when I was seeing Kevin again here, I . . . I don't agree with you about him. But in a way there's *nothing there*. At least he doesn't have the things I need. I think I've really known that for a long time now."

Lauren struck a match to her cigarette, finally, and drew on it deeply.

"Then why do you keep going back to him?"

"Because he's easier to be with than you are."

"Easy," I said carefully, "is not what it's all about."

"I know that," Lauren said. "And I'm not going to see him anymore."

I took a cigarette from the pack myself and lit it.

"You know, there's a funny thing about Kevin," I said. "I remember something that happened a long time ago when we were just out of school, kids practically, just beginning to learn the business. We were gofers on some cheapo flick and all of a sudden Kevin got a chance to boom. *Hands on the equipment*, man, that was a big deal to both of us then. Kevin had to hold a Sennhauser shotgun mike out at arm's length without moving it any. And he couldn't do it. He kept wobbling so the mike made noise, so then they gave it to me."

"What's funny about that?"

"Well, after about thirty seconds I thought my arm was going to fall off. And I knew my arm couldn't hold the mike out there any longer. That's when I learned something. It wasn't ever my arm that was going to do it anyway. My arm didn't even really need to exist. It was my will that was going to do everything. I don't think Kevin ever really learned that."

"My God, you make me so angry," Lauren said. "I'm not a prize in a pinball arcade. I'm not going to be a conquest. I am a sovereign human being. What you and Kevin do to each other doesn't matter to me that way."

"Okay," I said. "I should know that. I'm sorry."

"I want to stop fooling around now," Lauren said. "I want us to have a real marriage and I want it to work."

"Oh baby," I said, "you know I've always wanted that too," and then I had crossed to her chair and was kissing her face and mouth, until her grip on my shoulders turned from an embrace to a shove.

"Not now," she said. "I don't want to feel. I want to think."

I went back to the couch and sat heavily down.

"All right," I said. "What do you think?"

"I think it's going to be very hard for us," Lauren said. "It's strange, but it feels like the end."

"*Respice finem*," I said.

"What?"

"It *is* the end. It's the end of everything and the beginning of everything else."

We looked at each other. I said nothing and she said nothing and we stared at each other until I began to feel quite dizzy. I shook my head to clear it, and when I looked again I saw that Lauren's eyes were shut, and as a matter of fact she'd gone to sleep. Right then and there. It was amazing, really. Her lips were a little parted and her breathing was slow and deep. I could see her eyes moving back and forth below their closed lids, which meant, I suppose, that she was dreaming. I watched her reverently; it's hard not to fall in love with any quiet sleeper, and I loved Lauren so much already. Then she twitched a little and woke up.

"I want to go home," she said sleepily.

"You are home," I said, thinking she was only drowsy.

"Not here," she said. "Back to the farm."

"What for?" I said. "I never thought you liked it much. Why there?"

Lauren smiled and closed her eyes again, settling deeper into the chair.

"Because I'm pregnant."

After I had put her to bed, carefully, as if I were wrapping a Ming vase for storage, I left to take the train back uptown. I suppose it was a Freudian slip that made me overshoot the Sheridan Square stop and ride on to 14th Street, where Grogan's just happened to be. Trade in the bar was slow. There were two or three people on the stools besides me and a couple more asleep in the booths in the back. Terry nodded to me crabbily as he poured me my first drink. A beer and a shot and a beer and a shot. On the third round, the one he poured me free, I started crying. It wasn't that I was unhappy exactly, only that I'd had more than I could really absorb. I dropped my face into my folded arms to hide it.

A voice, not wholly familiar, spoke briefly in my head: *I'm bleeding to death and I don't even know it.*

Terry was shaking me by the shoulders. "No sleeping at the bar," he said.

I raised my head, obediently.

"What's the matter with you, then?" Terry said with some surprise.

What could I really tell him? My dog died?

"My wife left me," I said, knowing he'd prefer it kept simple.

"Ah, don't worry," Terry snarled, releasing my upper arms. "She'll come on back."

YOU MAY WELL ASK at this point, or soon, why, in view of Lauren's change of heart and my happy prospects of the restoration of my love and the renewal of my marriage and even the foundation of my family, why then didn't I just lay off the other project altogether. And the answer will be, I'm afraid, that I don't know. Of course there are the obvious reasons, prominent among them the point that there were a lot of other hungry people involved and there probably would have been precious little peace and contentment down on the farm if I didn't do something to satisfy them or otherwise calm them down. Then there was the simple momentum of the whole thing, which was already sweeping us all along with it, me very much included. But more even than that, I had a quite conscious sense that I would have to deliberately put an end to everything before everything else could properly begin.

Respice finem, indeed. Or you might just say that I didn't want to leave any unfinished business behind me. I myself will say nothing, because any sort of apology I could make would be too little and too late at this point.

But what it all immediately meant was that I had to pull

myself together and get out of Grogan's reasonably early and reasonably sober. I walked the long diagonal of Greenwich Avenue down to Sixth, where I could cross over to the Earle. In my room, I shook out the sheets and remade the bed, turned out the light and lay down. I needed to be as fresh as I could possibly manage the next day, so although at first I couldn't sleep, I didn't reach for the bottle or switch on the TV. I kept myself lying still in the dark, eyes closed, breathing deeply, listening to the tick-tock of my blood and feeling the alcohol roll out of my system like a tide.

Then it was four, four the next afternoon, and I had slept enough to get rested. I got up, washed and dressed, then went to the window and peered out. Yonko was on duty today.

Hell. I knew they'd be more careful now. The back door trick would never work on them twice in a row. I thought and I thought and then I had an idea. An absolutely simple idea. I checked the street again, picked up my shoulder bag, which was empty now, and went down to the desk. At my request the clerk called me a cab. When it arrived, I got in and rode away, leaving Yonko gaping on the sidewalk. It's only in the movies that there's always a second cab standing by, waiting to engage in hot pursuit at any moment.

I had the driver drop me at a midtown address where I could get an Aqualung. You can always get anything somewhere in New York, even if there's no obvious local use for whatever it is. I bought the gear outright and paid in cash. No cards, no names, no references. The tank was small and didn't take up much room in my bag, though it did add a lot of weight. I left the store and walked to where I could catch the F train downtown. At Delancey Street I changed for the J for Williamsburg.

It was rush hour now, and standing room only on the J train. I was packed into a mass of Puerto Ricans and Orthodox Jews for the most part, though there were enough other WASP invaders so that I didn't attract any special attention. I fought my way to a pocket against the connecting door of my car and when the train came clear of the tunnel and began to climb the bridge I stepped through it. The train turned and I swayed, unbalanced by the extra weight in my bag. The door slammed shut behind me and I caught the handles and braced myself back against it.

Fifty-dollar fine if I was caught, but I didn't really care. There was a raw visceral rush of speed as the train roared up the grade, cleaner and purer than any drug, and I gave myself up to it, until the bridge began to level off and the train slowed down. I looked between my feet, between the cars, to where the slow water of the East River blinked dully back up at me. Then I remembered what I was doing there and I looked to the north, stooping to peer under the steel I-beam that whizzed by at eye level, to see the low Brooklyn waterfront, the eastern shore.

There. Between the Pfizer tower and the Domino sugar factory, the *Eleusis* rode at anchor. Just as the shipping news had promised. She seemed as unmoving as the buildings behind her, as solid and secure. Sweet mystery. I bent over and cupped my hands to light a cigarette. So far, so very good.

Then the train braked and began to descend the far end of the bridge. A transit cop came out of the car opposite, plucked the cigarette out of my mouth and flipped it into the water without even looking at my face, and brushed by me into the next car. He didn't write me a summons or pull my I.D., which under all the circumstances meant I was getting off extremely lucky, so I contained my irritation. I wedged my way back into the car and when the train pulled into the first station I got off.

Now the thing was to stay clear of my own little former neighborhood, where somebody might conceivably recognize me. I went north on Havemeyer Street, where I was not known. At a hardware store there I stopped and bought a small block and tackle and some lightweight high-test nylon cord. There was still plenty of time to kill before nightfall and I doubled back toward Kent Avenue and the waterfront.

A good way north, twenty or twenty-five blocks from the bridge, in the middle of the warehouse district on Kent Avenue, there was still an old waterfront bar open, and that was where I went. It faced the river across a vacant lot and so caught the best of the sunset. I sat down at the table by the window, pushing my bag down underneath it. The bar was tended by an elderly Polish lady, who knew me by sight perhaps but not by name. I bought a tall can of beer and let it sit in front of me for an hour, two hours, more. The only other customers were a couple of truck drivers and a few of the withered emaciated prostitutes who walked Kent Avenue to serve them. I outlasted them all. I didn't drink or even smoke a cigarette. I sat staring across the river at the Empire State Building, and beyond it, the sun. Every so often the bartender shuffled across the room to draw the blind a little farther down, moving the bar of sunlight farther from me on the table. At length the shaft of light dropped from the table to the floor. An hour later, it was dark.

I went back south on Kent Avenue till I reached the break in the line of warehouses at the end of Grand Street, where there had been a halfhearted attempt to build a park. There were a few benches, a sad picnic table or two on the graveled surface, and a pervasive gaseous stench. I walked out on the pile of rocks that tipped into the water. There, down to my left, I could see the stern of the *Eleusis*, exactly where I'd planned for her to be.

I picked my way back across the rocks, sat down on the nearest bench, and slung my bag up on the table that came with it. My hand brushed something there which when I picked it up and felt it and examined it in silhouette against the faint light of Manhattan turned out to be a set of works, too dull to use again. *Works, works*, they call to you on the street. I remembered the forest of dropped needles in that

Roman park, and I remembered the film and several other things as well. Of course, this also was a needle park, when it was used at all. I threw the syringe in the direction of the river and unzipped my bag.

Then I saw the flaw, the gap, the lesion in my planning. I'd forgotten a thing or two, hadn't even brought a swimming suit, though that was a small problem. What was worse was that I had no partner, no one to watch my back, so that I'd have to leave some stuff exposed on the shore while I was underwater, and I'd be terribly exposed myself when I came out, lugging a heavy weight of the very thing the people most likely to turn up in this neighborhood would kill and die for. Kevin should have been there with me, but that wasn't in the cards. I sat there, my fingers curved to the cold rondure of the air tank, until I felt equally cold, equally mechanical. It was an uncalculated risk, to be sure, but I would just have to take it as such. I'd cut myself into this scene a long time before and there was nothing left to do now but just let it run through the sprockets.

So it seemed for the next strange few minutes to be not actually me at all who stripped to his underwear and put on the tank and the mask and the awkward swim fins. It was as though I were watching some other man pick up the sealed lamp I'd bought earlier that day and lurch over the rocks and down into the water, like some movie monster returning to the swamp, moving slowly and then deliberately until its head sinks from view. Then it was me again, sinking, alone and a little frightened in the dark.

I flicked on the lamp and began to swim. The East River water was so murky that the lamp was nearly useless. It had the sort of blanking effect that headlights do on fog. So I ran against the hull of the *Eleusis* before I had really seen it, and found my way forward to the bow mostly by touch. I measured my way back by arm spans and located that row of rivets at the water line. Counting, I swam down, my fingers on the bolts, *fifteen, twenty, twenty-one*, and nothing. Nothing, the load had gone to the sharks after all, and I drifted a little away from the hull, breathless, as though the tank had been ripped off my back and I were really drowning. Then I remembered: of course, the ship's draft would have been constantly changing as she was loaded and unloaded, so I swam farther down, not counting anymore but only following the line of rivets, and then I found it.

The metal mesh that covered the load was still secure, the lamp showed me, and I went to work slowly, shifting the powerful magnets inch by inch, loosening the package until I could grasp it and draw it out. It had a hook to attach to my harness, but I'd brought no harness, another oversight. I let the lamp go then, its light fading quickly as it sank, and hugging the package to my chest, I kicked away from the ship. It wasn't far; I swam a few dozen yards maybe, estimating, and let myself float to the surface at what turned out to be a perfectly safe distance from the bank. Compared to underwater the night seemed very bright and I saw at once that the park was still vacant. Clutching the package to me, I swam in to shore.

Of course I hadn't thought to bring a towel either, so I just had to stay wet. Though the water had been warm I was cold enough once I stood up, soaking, in the light breeze that came across the river from the city. More alarming was the tingling, not quite a burning sensation yet, all over my body, which I took to come from the acid content of the river water.

Trembling, I stripped off my shorts and put on my pants and shirt, which lay clammily against my wet limbs. I pushed the rubber-sheathed load and the scuba gear into my bag and left the park, headed north on Kent Avenue now, toward the bridge. I was still dripping wet and I knew I must look very peculiar, but it was not a neighborhood where much attention would be paid to that and in any case I met no one walking along the waterfront. At the bridge I turned east and walked three or four blocks along the supporting wall, to reach the entrance to the walkway. By then the wind had blown me nearly dry, but I was still shaking a little, possibly from nerves.

The broken rail had not been repaired since my last visit to the bridge. I set the bag down near the gap and took out the load. That was the difficult point, the moment when it would have been so easy to peel back the waterproofing and have just a little blast. And maybe fill my pockets up for later . . . The prospect froze me on the spot for five minutes, maybe ten, but in the end I didn't do it. Instead I began climbing the stanchions, calling up acrobatic abilities I wasn't sure I had. I arranged the rope over the pulleys and hauled the package up into the shadows, out of my reach and sight.

A temporary solution, but I believed it would hold for a couple of hours' worth of nighttime. I dropped back onto the metal plates of the walkway and retrieved my shoulder bag. The Aqualung would be of no use to me anymore, I knew, and it wasn't a good idea to hang on to it. I wrapped the hose and the flippers around the tank and heaved it all spinning out over the bridge rail. If there was any splash I didn't hear it. My bag empty again now, I walked down into the city.

Grushko and Yonko were both covering the Earle tonight. I came in through the park and slipped up on them from behind. From the way they whipped around I could tell that they were ready.

"Tonight," I said, and nothing more. Grushko nodded stiffly. Yonko, aiming his shopping bag at my torso, didn't respond at all.

I went into the hotel and rode the elevator up to my floor, inspecting myself in the convex triangular mirror in the upper corner of the car. My hair was matted from the dive, but otherwise I thought I looked no different than usual. In my room I took a long soapy shower, scrubbing my skin until that last acid tingling was gone. I threw away my wet clothes and put on fresh ones, then went back down to the street.

The Bulgarians were gone, as I'd expected. There was time to spare so I began walking: down to Houston, over to the Bowery, down to Delancey Street, over to the bridge. It was past midnight and the area was abandoned, all the shops along the street locked down and shuttered for the night. At a pay phone on the corner of Clinton I dialed Kevin's number. It was my last piece of uncourted good luck that I got him and not his machine.

"Early delivery," I said. "Same place, tonight, right now. You've got thirty minutes, then it's gone."

I hung up before he could say anything and crossed to the island in the middle of Delancey Street, opposite the stairway to the bridge. Waiting for the light, I scanned the area carefully, but there seemed to be no one around, which was all to the good. At ground level inside the stone stairwell there was a broken door behind which someone could have hidden, but the door was ajar and there was no sound or movement from the space behind it. No one was loitering around the rail at the head of the stairs either. I began to climb the bridge. Halfway up the ramp I turned back and looked again but there was still no one and nothing to see.

It was twenty minutes later, maybe twenty-five, when I saw a shadow slip between the bars on the walkway where the metal superstructure started. I'd climbed the girders again and braced myself in a joint about ten feet above the walk. I watched the shadow approach me, growing larger, until it resolved itself into Kevin. He must have taken a cab to get there so quickly and I wondered, without too much concern, if he could have persuaded the driver to wait. But the main thing was that I seemed to have caught him flatfooted by moving up the date. As I'd hoped, he hadn't had time to round up any semi-silent partners or other extra people, and so he'd come alone.

When he got a little closer I saw that he was wearing glasses, small round lenses with wire frames. The glasses made him look vulnerable somehow, or maybe it was only the idea of his needing them. Kevin was wary, I could tell; he kept swinging his head from side to side, peering into every shadow, but he walked with his usual light confidence. Then he was almost directly under me, beside the broken rail.

"Heads up," I said in a normal speaking tone.

It was maybe the first time, I thought, I'd ever seen him really startled.

"Good God," he said. "Isn't this a little wild and hairy? Why don't you swing down out of there and we'll talk like human beings."

I shook my head. "Rules of the game."

"Whose rules? What game?"

"Don't know. Not yours this time, that's all."

Kevin shook his head with exaggerated disgust.

"All right," he said. "Now what?"

"Will you take delivery?"

"What, do you want a receipt?"

"Stand back a little, then."

Kevin backed up, closer to the edge of the walkway now, and I reached up and pulled loose the bow knot I'd tied in the nylon cord. The line whistled over the pulleys and then the load slammed into the walkway, perfect targeting, right in front of Kevin's feet.

"Bravo," Kevin said, looking down and then smiling up at me. "Bravissimo."

"Thanks," I said. "I try."

But Kevin was no longer paying attention. He was working away at the wrapping, going in for a sample taste, bent over the bag, his full concentration on it. Without planning to I vaulted off my stanchion and landed in a crouch, saving my balance with one hand. Kevin glanced up.

"Back to earth, eh?" he said, and went back to the package. I walked toward him slowly, not thinking, but with my hypothalamus screaming wordlessly. *Do it now.* There was nothing back of Kevin but the river. Then, with more speed than I would have given him credit for, he stood up, glancing behind him and to the side. I came on, a little slower. A click and a flash, and Kevin had a knife in his right hand.

I stopped, bewildered; Kevin didn't carry weapons, but I had a maddening certainty I'd seen that knife before. Then I knew it was not déjà vu at all but memory of that night at the Empire. The knife had been in my hand then and I had given it to Kevin. Of course, of course. A knife cuts friendship. Now both of us were free.

Kevin, who might have been having a similar thought, was now moving in on me. I moved my feet for a fighting stance, though I still left my hands low. Kevin kept coming, stepping over the package, the knife extended before him like a fencing foil.

"I wouldn't," I said. "Maybe you can't take me even with the knife."

"Maybe."

I raised my hands a little.

"It's enough. You like sure things, Kevin, both of us know that."

Kevin stopped, threw back his head and laughed. It comforts me a little now to remember him laughing then.

"Ah, what the hell, Tracy, what the hell. It's all been a little tense, hasn't it." And he spread his arms out wide. For just one second I had a mad impulse to run to him, accept the bear hug, take him somewhere and buy him a drink . . . Then I saw how it would happen, how when he closed his arms the knife would slide into my back. Maybe it would only be an accident, maybe he'd forget he still had it in his hand.

"Sure," I said, remaining where I was, unmoving, unblinking. Kevin shrugged and backed away, the knife still in front of him, stepping surely back over the package without needing to look down. He stooped and gathered the package under his left arm and backed off toward Manhattan now, still pointing the knife my way. I stood still. Kevin made about twenty or twenty-five yards and then he called to me.

"It's tough sometimes, you know how it is," he said with another shrug, shifting his grip on the package. "Don't follow me." He must have thought the distance was safe enough because he turned then and went on.

But I did follow him. Not very close and not very far, but once he'd passed through the bars at the end of the metal section of the walk, I went up to the junction point and waited. Though he seemed to look back over his shoulder a time or two, I doubt he saw me standing there. I watched him until he vanished into the stairwell and then I found myself counting under my breath, against my will. The time passed very slowly, slowly enough for me to think that every guess I'd made was wrong, long enough for a sort of relief to begin to settle in. Then I heard it: the opening rattle of the machine guns, first one and then the other, muffled and much softer than I'd expected, like voices answering each other in a conversation overheard from another room. It seemed not to concern me at all, that conversation; I felt no connection to it, believed fully then that it had all come about simply through *choc en retour*. So I felt no responsibility and certainly no fear, not even the least nervousness about continuing to stand there through the long silence that followed the end of the firing, that silence which was finally closed off by the first high lonesome wailing of the sirens.

20

WE'VE BEEN BACK at the farm for a little over a month now, and so far I can say that things are going quite well. Better, perhaps, than I have any right to expect. In the beginning I was nervous and jumpy and had an irresistible urge to keep looking back over my shoulder. One of the first things I did was clean all the guns and spread them handily around the house, unloaded but with shells conveniently nearby. Lauren was sure to have noticed that but she said nothing to me about it. And nothing has come of it. Last week I collected the guns and put them all back in the rack upstairs. Grushko and Yonko must be either satisfied or else unable to find me. I believe now that they've been absorbed, one way or another, back into the urban miasma, them and their knapsack full of dope, and I don't worry about them anymore.

Everything here was much as I had left it, a little dustier in the house, a little more overgrown outdoors. A note left by my tenant detailed births and deaths among the sheep. There were a few calls on my machine but nothing of particular importance. The package from Heathrow had made it through, even though the address wasn't totally accurate. It sat on the porch beside the front door, a little rain-splattered and with one corner torn, sagging inside its cord. The label directed it to my maternal great-grandfather, but he's been dead for so many years I didn't feel bad about opening it.

Another one of the first things I did was take that half-full bottle of bourbon, still waiting for me on the bread board there, and pour it down the sink. It was a wrench to do it, but I did. Lauren has not commented on this either, but I think she's noticed and is pleased. Oh, someday, I'm sure, I'll have another drink, but not today.

It's fall now; the leaves are turning and withering from the limbs. Though there's nothing really here to harvest I manage to stay busy. I've mown the front pasture and the field on the hill. I keep the yard well raked and trimmed, and lately I've been trying to fix some of the fences, though that's not something I know a lot about. There's satisfaction in this work; beyond the fact that it fills my days, there's the pleasure that I learn to take in the ordinary. More than anything I want to be ordinary now, to discover the savor of each particular: the smell of the wood, ringing of the nails, weight of the hammer in my hand. I have come to believe that this dailiness may save me.

We don't go out much now. Lauren doesn't seem to crave company, which is just as well, since I know few people around here nowadays. Most nights I cook our supper and she praises it, a small flattery which pleases me inordinately. She sleeps a lot, and seems happy enough to read or putter around the house when she's awake; she keeps the house in better order than it's been in for a long time. There are a lot of books here; some, she tells me, that she's always meant to read. Her pregnancy is beginning to show a little, not so much in her belly as in the rounding and softening of her face and arms.

It is the calmest time we've known together, and it seems, deceptively, too easy. It must be harder, and one day soon enough I'm sure it will be. It seems to be my luck to see things structurally, and I picture our first greedy love as a sort of core, an inner ring, a spot where something fell and started ripples. At night as I am absorbed into sleep I sometimes picture it as if I were the original stone itself, spiraling into darkness, while above I see not waves but expanding radiant bands of light.

Wheels within wheels within wheels. I think we are trying to find our way out into the higher concentricity of which Kierkegaard writes, which I still read about in the evenings. A dizzyingly distant prospect at times. I believe, because I have to, that love can become full trust and faith without being any the less love.

All the same I don't sleep well. Some node swells up behind my eyes and bursts into a flash of light; I wake up breathless and amazed that I am staring at the dark. It gets a little tiresome. I'll lie there, for more than an hour sometimes, and cue and review the whole mental reel, all of the things that have happened. It must be that I am looking for some place it can be cut, but there is none, not even in imagination. In the end there's little use in such reflection, myself upon myself upon myself. Nothing can be changed or rearranged.

Make of it what you will.

Last night, at around the time I'd usually pick to pour a drink, I went out into the yard. The sky was clear and the stars were bright, though they looked cold and distant from me. (It's getting chilly at night now, cool enough for fires.) I had a strong sensation that someone was watching me, so that I turned around, but I found nothing there. I still wanted to check behind myself, to look and keep on looking, but I controlled the impulse.

It was peculiar how the feeling stayed with me, that someone or something was watching. Someone who knew what I had done and didn't like it. Something that disapproved.

I dreamed I was climbing a high mountain in a fog. Strapped to my back was a baby, which I knew was my child and Lauren's. And yet the baby was not a real infant at all but a tiny wise old man wrapped up in swaddling clothes. More knowledgeable by far than I, he directed me where to put my feet so that we should not fall.

When I began to emerge from the dream it was still dark. I tried to picture the wise child again but the only face that came was Kevin's, Kevin's head spliced to an infant body in a last absurd chameleon change.

"Why did you kill me?" his voice said, and then I was fully awake and staring at the dark spot on the ceiling where the image seemed to have been.

It was true.

I killed you, there's no quibbling about it, it wasn't poetic justice or anything else. I killed you, old friend, old enemy, but I never could have done it without your help.

Today I got another dog. I drove down to Hickman County where I know a breeder and paid a princely sum for a black and tan Doberman puppy, his tail bobbed but his ears untrimmed, still floppy like a hound's. Beside me on the car seat, he gnawed my fingers all the way back to the farm, and each needle-sharp twinge tightened his spell on me.

I'd gone down there on impulse and hadn't warned Lauren. She was surprised, a little annoyed, but finally charmed. I swore I'd be responsible for his training. With the financial success of my recent ventures it will be a while before I need to work again. I will have time and to spare to train a puppy. So Lauren resigned herself to the dog. So much so that in the end she wanted to take him to bed with her, and I had to draw the line at that. The puppy sleeps now in a box lined with newspaper here beside the stove.

I am quite looking forward to the uncomplicated relationship I began with this dog today. There's a lot that I will teach him, and as much I won't and can't. He'll never learn to tell lies or withhold information. Sins of commission or omission will be meaningless to him. He will never know either guilt or doubt, which gives him tremendous advantages over me.

There remain things that Lauren and I have not said to one another and probably never will. It is a sort of unspoken pact between us which neither of us can refer to. She will not ask me any questions about Kevin, though I have no doubt she knows that I could answer some. And I will not ask her which one of us is the father of our child.

How stable such complicity can be I can't predict. Though for now we're happy in each other, I can't be certain how long that will last. Lauren may lose the peace she's found these weeks, may find the urge to wander overcoming her again. Or it may be me who somehow breaks our circle.

The future can't be guaranteed.

All the same, when in a few more minutes I shut off the lights and follow her to bed, I will believe that what we've started is enough. I will believe that this immediacy can become a permanence. By force of my desire and will I'll make this time a fortress for the future. We'll curl together against the cold and hold each other safe till morning.

What child will be born of this union, I do not know.